SAFE

AT

HOME

BY

PAULA BOTT

Scobre Press Corporation
2255 Calle Clara
La Jolla, CA 92037

Scobre Press books may be purchased for
educational, business or sales promotional use.

Edited by Ramey Temple
Illustrated by James Mellett
Cover Design by Michael Lynch

ISBN 1-933423-99-4

HOME RUN EDITION

www.scobre.com

CHAPTER ONE

THE FIELD

"Get in a line everyone. Let's pick 'em." My brother Joe pointed and shouted. He tried to organize the group of noisy boys around him. "Let's move, the sun goes down in two hours."

Playing and winning on "the Field" meant everything to us back then. Most of the neighborhood kids would find their way to the Field every day. We'd play for hours. If enough kids showed up, we'd play real games. Some nights, we'd stay out until the sky was nearly black. The bright Arizona moon would be the only light shining down on us.

The Field was a strip of beat-up grass located right next to our apartment. Most of our free time was spent there, even though it was in such poor condition. The area was about one quarter the size of a football field, and it wasn't well cared for. Weeds

1

poked through the grass and big rocks jutted out everywhere.

I lived in the town of Tierra de Sueño, which, in Spanish means *dreamland*. Five of us shared a second floor apartment, located behind a tall wooden fence. That same fence acted as the left field foul line on the Field. Hitting one over the fence counted as an automatic out. Balls hit there were rarely found. They always ended up buried deep in the bushes.

I usually played center field and I loved it. My heart would race when I'd catch a line drive in the webbing of my glove or chase down a fly ball. The pothole-filled outfield was a tough place to run. Twisted ankles and bloody knees were not uncommon. Still, it was a safer place to play than the infield. Out here, players could avoid one-hoppers and line drives. Not that I was scared of them. I would have played shortstop or first base in a second. I got stuck in center because of my age, and because I was a girl. Only the older boys brought their gloves into the infield. Ground balls on the Field bounced around like they were inside a pinball machine.

While the brave ones lined up in the infield, only the best players lined up in right. This part of the Field included a section of our street. This was the one spot where errors weren't tolerated. Right fielders on the Field had to guard parked cars from flying baseballs. That job often included leaning your hip on a car's side door. A bad play from a right fielder could result in disaster. Cracked windshields and dented doors ended more than a few of our games. I was the youngest player *and* the only female. Still, I never worried about getting left off a team. In terms of skills, I was right about in the middle of the pack. When captains chose teams I was never picked last. My oldest brother, Jose, who we called Joe, organized most of the games. He would usually stick me on his team in center field anyway. I was a short and skinny nine-year-old girl, but I was athletic and tough. I had the cuts and bruises to prove it. Being the underdog made me fight twice as hard.

On this particular day, I wasn't even given the chance to compete. Home Run Derby was the game of the day. Joe, my know-it-all brother, pushed me away. He stuck out his bony chest and raised his chin, his jet-black hair shining. "Sorry, Selena, today is only for the big boys. Maybe tomorrow." He turned to the crowd of boys. "Come on guys, line up and let's pick'em."

I looked over at Carlos, my older brother. I was hoping he'd say something. Carlos usually treated me more gently than Joe. Out on the Field, though, he went along with Joe's tough-guy attitude. The fact that Carlos was thirty pounds lighter than our big brother had something to do with this. My next option was to run home and tell Mom. I knew she would make it all right. But she was working downtown. I didn't know what to do. My mind raced. I stared at the big rock that sat on the edge of the Field. It acted as a back-stop for our bizarre shaped diamond. The boulder towered over me. It had a crease in it's side that looked like a set of big lips.

The boys formed the line that Joe had commanded. From there, they began to choose teams. I jumped up on top of the big rock behind them. I sat down on it and dangled my feet over the side. The boys continued to pick teams. I tried to think of a way to get into the game. A few of the boys below me looked up to see what I was doing. I twisted my black hair around my index finger. With each thought my short legs swung faster and faster. *I got it!* I thought. I knew the perfect way to make sure that I would get a chance to play.

I pushed myself off the rock, landing feet first in a thick clump of grass. The boys still tried to ignore me. That is, until I made a challenge that changed everything. "I bet I can hit the ball farther than you, Joe." I spoke loudly, pointing at him in front of everyone. This comment drew the attention of the entire crowd. "Well?" I said, putting my hands on my hips.

"Ooooh." Sergio Lopez shot a sharp look at my brother. "Now that's a challenge, Joe." He was egging him on.

"You get one pitch and I get three," I continued. "If I lose, I won't bug you to let me play ever again. If I win, from now on, I always get to play."

After I had spoken those words I wanted them

back. What if Joe hit the ball farther than me? He *was* the best player on the Field. If I lost, would I ever get the chance to play on the Field again? I had to take back my offer. "Wait, Joe, I—"

"See, I knew it," he said. "Now you're being smart, Selena. You don't want to play against me."

His cocky attitude made me want to scream. I couldn't back down now. "Yes I do." I moved closer to my brother. "Unless, I mean—" I grinned.

"Unless what?" He asked.

"Unless you're too scared—too chicken." I raised my eyebrows at my brother and laughed as I said, "Are you too chicken, Joe?"

Sergio looked over at him and started flapping his arms up and down. "Buck, buck, buck, buck, buck!" I heard a few other boys jump in. I could see that Joe was angry now.

I smiled as I twisted the ribbons and bows Mom had put in my hair. This was something Mom and I did every day. Each morning before school, she would take the time to put ribbons and bows in my hair. Every time I got nervous or excited about something I would run my fingers through them.

"Buck, buck, buck, buck, buck." Carlos joined Sergio.

"Shut up!" Joe shot a mean look over at Carlos. He then moved closer to me, whispering so that only I could hear him. "Okay, Selena, but just remember, you asked for this. It's time I teach you a lesson, little girl." Joe glanced at the crowd. "Let's play ball." He smiled nervously again. He knew that this was not a winning situation for him. On one hand, he couldn't turn down my challenge. He had to accept it. But even if he beat his baby sister, he would still look foolish.

There was also the unthinkable—he *could* lose.

Feeling the pressure, Joe spoke to the crowd once more. "I'll even bat left-handed, to give her a chance." Everyone smiled at this show of sportsmanship. The truth was, they were all hoping that the biggest and oldest boy on the Field would lose.

I reached down and grabbed the smallest bat. Being the youngest had one advantage—I got to go first. I dug my dirty white tennis shoes into the ground. "I'm ready," I yelled. The group of boys stood a few feet behind me at home plate. Joe made his way to the pitcher's mound.

He lofted the first pitch softly in the air. My uppercut swing sent the baseball looping high, but not far. That wasn't going to do it. Even left-handed, my brother would be able to hit the ball farther than that. "That was just the first one." I explained to the crowd. "Give me another one, Jose."

The second pitch was inside, and the ball weakly bounced off the handle of my bat. It was even shorter than my first swing. Joe was really smiling now. He was about to beat me very easily—*and* do so left-handed. "All right, this is it. Now I'm serious." I tried to convince myself. The crowd settled back a few feet. They were disappointed by my first two swings. *Keep your eye on the ball, Selena,* I told myself. Snapping the bat back into position, I stared at Joe's right hand. His next pitch came in low. This forced me to level out my swing. As I extended my short arms, the ball hit the "sweet spot" of my bat. I knew I'd hit it well just by the way it sounded. Smack! It shot forty feet in the air, sailing deep into center field. It was probably the farthest ball I had ever hit.

"Whoooa!" reacted the neighborhood boys who stood behind me.

"Uh-oh, Joe." Sergio laughed and looked over at my brother.

"Big hit, Selena!" Carlos slapped me five.

I raised my right arm and pointed at the ball. "I think that's a winner!"

The smirk on Joe's face showed his nervousness. He tried to mask it, lifting his head high. "Give me any bat. It doesn't matter."

Sergio tossed him the big barrel. "Show us what you've got, Joe."

Joe flipped the bat over his left shoulder. Each of his practice swings sent the giant bat wobbling in different directions. He was no switch-hitter. Everyone knew that.

"Remember, only one swing," I laughed.

All eyes focused on Joe. Carlos wound up and delivered a pitch in the dirt. Joe was smart enough not to swing at that one. "Sorry Joe," Carlos winked at me. He was doing whatever he could to help me win. I knew that his next pitch would have to be a strike or he'd really hear it from Joe. Sure enough, I was right. Carlos let go of a straight pitch that headed right down the middle. As the ball reached the batter's box Joe swung with all his might. He connected. At first, I thought his ball was going to fly past mine. Luckily, the ball smacked the top half of his bat. This caused it to sail straight up into the air. It plopped down near second base, well short of my blast.

"That was a terrible pitch!" Joe yelled as he walked up to Carlos and gave him a shove.

I skipped over to Joe to shake his hand. He walked away from me. "Go away, Selana."

My light brown face beamed anyway. "Looks like I'll be seeing you guys tomorrow, and the next day, and the next day, and the next."

The fact that I had earned an automatic invite to play was great. But the greatest prize I earned that day on the Field was respect. After seeing me take on Joe, everyone agreed that this little girl could play. I stopped hearing whispers of, "Just let her get on base." The "pitch underhand to Selena" rule was wiped out, too. Now that I was officially "one of the guys," baseball became the focus of my life. Winning that bet with Joe started it all. From that day forward—more than anything else—I wanted to be a baseball player.

CHAPTER TWO

A HARD CALL

"Cup check! Cup check!" As a member of the Pirates Little League team, I'd listened to that for twelve straight weeks.

Before every game, Coach Fisher would walk by each boy and yell from above him: "Cup check! Cup check!" One by one my teammates would stand up and knock on their cups. When he'd reach me, the only girl on a boys' team, he'd stop. Instead of screaming "cup check," he'd yell, "gut check!" It sounds silly, but it got me fired up.

Getting permission from Mom and Dad to be the only girl on an all-boys team wasn't easy. It took awhile, but Dad eventually caved in. After a month of begging, he signed me up to play baseball with the boys.

Mom wasn't quite as thrilled. She wanted me

to play softball. Mom was sure that I would get more enjoyment from competing against and hanging out with girls. But I had no interest in Bobby Sox softball. Especially after what Terry Silva told me about their practices. Their coaches actually put little pink stickers on the softballs. They did this so the girls would concentrate while batting. Any league where the players *forgot* to concentrate was not for me. I was an athlete, not some pink princess.

As it turned out, competing against the boys wasn't a problem for me. Growing up with two older brothers made me tougher than most of them anyway. So despite being the only she-Pirate, I became one of our best players. My hitting really took off now that I was playing on a regular-sized baseball diamond. Unlike the strange measurements of the Field, my deep shots to left and right field were now fair game. I also became great with my glove. I easily predicted the baseball's hops on the nice fields we played on. Tracking fly balls became easier, too—I no longer had to jump over potholes and in between cars.

To be honest, Mom *was* right about one thing. The social part of being on an all-boys team wasn't so great. The talk in the dugout centered around video games, comic books, and skateboards. None of these things interested me. Even if they had, the boys would not have included me in their talks. I don't know why, but having me around bothered some of them. It was hard, but I tried not to take offense to their dirty looks and mean comments. Instead, I focused on playing baseball.

This was my attitude going into our final game against the Dodgers. Aside from us, they were the only other undefeated team in the league. This meant that today's winning team would be the league champion. The crowd of Pirates ran to their positions as the game got underway. Garret Carter found his spot in right field. Dennis Martinez jumped up and down on third base. I sprinted over to first, the position I had played the entire season.

A heavy wind blew across the field. Tommy Johnson's hat was knocked from his head. I never had to worry about losing my cap. Mom pulled my long black hair through the back of my hat each game. As usual, she tied my ponytail using bright yellow ribbon—which matched our yellow and black uniforms.

During the past three months, I'd become one of the best first basemen in the league. Coach said that I was a natural at scooping up short hops. I knew better. The truth was, there was nothing natural about it. I'd been practicing those scoops since second grade on the beat-up grass of the Field. Swallowing up bad throws on the perfectly kept infields I now played on was easy.

The game got under way. A pop-up and a strikeout retired the first two Dodgers to start the inning. I punched the center of my mitt, cheering on our pitcher, Mark Bedford. "Here we go, Mark, right down the pipe, Mark. No batter, no batter, no batter, no batter, no batter." Just as I finished my sentence, their number three hitter whacked one. The one-hopper was heading right for Tommy at second base. He was able to knock it down but his throw floated to the left side of first base. Right away I knew I couldn't stretch my glove that far across my body. I reacted with pure instinct, reaching out my bare right hand to stop the ball. My index finger snapped backward as the ball smacked into my palm. Luckily, it dropped straight down, keeping the runner from advancing to second. I shook my stinging hand, hoping the pain would disappear.

Coach Fisher started to walk out of the dugout to check on my condition. I waved him off with my glove. "I'm fine," I shouted.

"You sure?" he answered back from the dugout's top step.

I nodded, not wanting to show my pain with a cracked voice. As I bowed my head, I remembered all the times I'd been banged up on the Field. I even remembered a few barehanded catch attempts. I never quit on my neighborhood turf, and I wasn't going to quit here.

I bent down, placing both hands on my knees. A moment later, the fourth batter hit a slow roller back to our pitcher. I looked back at the first base bag and ran toward it. Then I planted my right foot on the corner of the white square. Jacob tossed a bullet into the heart of my glove. Three outs.

I ran into the dugout and dropped my glove on the ground. Shaking off my stinging hand, I headed straight for the water cooler. The fresh water relieved my dry throat. Once I was out of the view of my teammates, I splashed some on my hand.

Unfortunately, Jacob saw me. "Did you break a fingernail, Selena?" he teased. The rest of the boys laughed.

"Did you forget you had a glove?" chimed in Dennis.

I rolled my eyes, turning my attention to the action on the field. This was the way they'd teased me all year long. When it first started, I would yell and scream back at them. Eventually, I realized that my reaction was fueling their fire. The more I yelled, the more obnoxious they became. About halfway through the season Dad sat me down for a conversation. He explained that the boys' words were dripping with jealousy. After all, I was a girl, and I was better than most of them. *I* knew my barehanded stop was a great play. So I didn't need to respond to their stupid comments.

Although my teammates would never admit it, I was the best hitter we had. By the sixth inning, I had reached base safely in every at-bat. In the third, I hit a two-run homer to left field—my sixth that season.

We led 6-5 going into the top half of the seventh, the final inning. The Dodgers had one chance remaining. The first Dodger hit a pop-up right into the glove of our third baseman. The next guy walked on four straight pitches. He then moved over to second on a wild pitch. With one out, their best hitter, Andy Newsome, stepped to the plate. He pulled his undersized royal blue shirt over his round belly. Then he stared toward center field. He was big and strong, a kid who crushed the ball when he connected. We all took a step back.

On the first pitch, Andy barely made contact with the ball. His grounder to our shortstop, David Gonzalez, surprised everyone. The ball bounced off the heel of David's glove and rolled toward the pitcher's mound. David hustled after it. When he reached the ball, he threw off-balance toward the left side of first base. The speeding ball skipped hard into the dirt. I was able to stretch to my left and reach my glove down to scoop up the short hop. Thanks to some flexibility, my foot managed to stay on the rubber base too. Stretching for a tough scoop was one of the hardest plays for a first baseman.

I was excited, and started to stand upright after completing the second out. Right when I lifted my head, though, I knew I was about to get creamed. Andy was chugging down the line as fast as he could. He tried to stop himself, but couldn't. Instead, he slammed into me with his massive shoulder. Giant Andy rolled over me like a truck smacking into an empty garbage can. When the dust settled, I was flat on my back. I struggled to get to my feet, but couldn't. The umpire ran over to us to get a closer look. Just as he arrived, I extended my left hand high into the air. I was dazed, but I'd still secured the ball in my glove. Andy was called out!

Before I had the chance to celebrate, I noticed something from the corner of my eye. The Dodger's runner, who'd started on second, was now heading home. Still sitting on the infield dirt, I spun around on my butt. I snatched the ball out of my glove and threw home with all my might. Although I was throwing from an awkward position, the ball zipped straight toward the plate. Our catcher, Thad Hudson, caught it and tagged the runner for the final out.

Game over! Pirates win!

Coaches from both teams ran over to the crash site at first base. Andy and I both stood up, shaking the dust from our uniforms. Once standing, I reflected on the most exciting play I'd ever made on a baseball field. I couldn't help but smile through the pain I was feeling. Coach Fisher bent down and put his arm around me. "Talk about a gut check. What a play! You okay, Selena?"

"Yeah, I'm fine, Coach," I lied. The *truth* was, Giant Andy had bruised my leg pretty bad. Plus, I'd bit my tongue when I hit the ground. I could taste the blood in my mouth. There was no way I was going to let my teammates see that I was hurt, though. I stood up and walked off the field. A group of cheering parents gave me a round of applause.

The boys ignored my great play, of course. Dennis was the first to pick on me. "It looked like Andy was trying to kiss you," he smiled. I wasn't surprised. Upset, yes, but not surprised. I had just won us the game, yet none of my teammates had anything nice to say.

After we shook hands with the other team, I sprinted over to the stands. Mom walked towards me, her lawn chair under her left arm. She'd been to all of my games this season. Dad worked late hours so he had only seen a few. I flipped my duffel bag onto Mom's right arm. "Can you hold this for a second?" I bent down to tie my shoe.

Mom grabbed the bag with one hand. She looked like a catcher grabbing a wild pitch. "I'm so proud of you. Wow, what a great play!"

I lowered my head, showing my frustration. "Yeah, at least somebody noticed. I'm so sick of these boys. You should've heard all the stupid things they said to me today. The same junk I've heard all season."

Mom lifted up our dog, Campeóna, to my face. She gave me a big wet kiss on my ear and I started to laugh. Campeóna, which means *champion* in Spanish, had been my dog since I was five. Mom brought her to all my games as a good luck charm. Campeóna was a little white mutt who weighed about ten pounds.

While giving me a hug, Mom eyed my dusty ribbon. "Let me fix your hair." She carefully put down the bag and chair and retied the yellow ribbon.

"You're one tough cookie." A voice interrupted us. A short, balding man with a black goatee came up behind us. "That was a heck of a play."

I looked down, embarrassed by his compliment. "Thank you."

"Have you ever considered playing Bobby Sox softball? My two daughters have played the last couple of years. They really love it. I'm coaching an under-twelve team next year and we're looking for players. We'd sure love to have someone as good as you." The man could tell I was uncomfortable. Somehow, he sensed that I didn't want to give up baseball. His tone softened. "If you want, I'll get you the information. No pressure."

Mom looked at me and raised her eyebrows. I stared back at her, shrugging my shoulders in uncertainty. I was able to hold my own with the boys, but playing alongside them was no fun. I simply was not accepted. But *soft*ball? I wasn't sure.

"Here's my number." The man handed Mom a business card. "If you decide you want to play, give me a call."

"Thank you." Mom nodded her head in appreciation.

As the man faded in the distance Mom bumped my hip playfully with her hip. "What do you think?"

I wasn't exactly sure what I thought. Mom's eyes looked into mine. She was reading my mind and could tell I was deep in thought. I glanced at the base-ball diamond, at my muddied uniform, my glove and my hat. *Softball games are played on a diamond*, I thought. *You wear a glove too. And you can slide just as hard as you can in baseball.* A moment later, I fixed my eyes on some of my Pirate teammates. They were still making comments about me breaking a fin-gernail and wanting to kiss Andy. I realized exactly what I had to do. I turned my attention back to Mom. "Maybe we should give that guy a call."

On the car ride home I tried to convince myself that playing softball would be great. *It's just like base-ball*, I thought. *The ball is bigger and they pitch underhand instead of overhand. So what? I'll be able to hang out with girls. Maybe I'll even make some friends.*

CHAPTER THREE

A CHANGEUP

It was strange pulling on my first ever softball uniform. I didn't really like the neon orange and black color scheme. That was the bad news. The good news was that I'd gained something valuable when I joined the all-girls Bobby Sox softball league—comfort.

Switching from baseball to softball was a change I never expected to make. Once I did, though, I realized that it wasn't so bad. To start, I was more physically comfortable playing softball. Switching sports meant that I shed baseball's hot pants in favor of cool mesh shorts. I also dropped the short-sleeve jersey tops. In their place were relaxed, cotton tank tops. This had nothing to do with fashion. It had everything to do with the heat of Arizona. For that reason, comfort owned a top spot on my list of priorities.

The other major comfort factor was that I was

now hanging around girls. Finally, I had found a team where I fit in! Gone were the nasty comments I'd heard while playing baseball with the boys.

It didn't take long for me to adjust to playing with a softball. I followed Coach's advice and worked on placing my fingers on the laces. This gave my small hand a better grip on the larger ball. I also found out that playing first base was easier in softball. The ball was a bigger target for me to scoop and squeeze in my glove.

Switching sports drastically changed my hitting style. I quickly realized that smacking home runs was much harder in this sport. The ball didn't travel nearly as far as a baseball did. So I shortened my swing and stopped going for the fences. After a few weeks, I had changed into a reliable contact hitter. At the age of ten, I'd found my comfort zone in softball.

The biggest change in my game occurred during the second half of my first season. One day in practice, I was catching fly balls in the outfield. I was out there with Jamie Morrison, our star pitcher. She was sidelined with a broken leg. We were all bummed out for her.

A high fly ball landed directly in my glove. For some reason, I threw the ball back to home plate underhanded. The bullet hopped through the infield dirt with great speed. It bounced twice before reaching home plate. "Hey Selena, you're gonna hurt your arm throwing from out there." Coach Larry Shepard shouted in a raspy voice. He was the man who had recruited me for girl's softball in the first place.

I placed my hand on my hip. "Why don't you give me a chance on the mound then, Coach." I was joking, of course. I loved playing first base.

Apparently, Coach Shepard didn't get a joke when he heard one. A few moments later he was running toward the outfield grass. And he was holding a catcher's glove. When he reached me, he smiled. "If you're any good, this could really help us, Selena." He spoke excitedly through deep breaths. Coach paced off forty-five feet and crouched down in a catcher's stance. "Okay, show me what you've got."

My heart started to race as the entire team surrounded me. I gripped the ball in my hand and stared at the catcher's mitt. I'd watched Jamie pitch before and I pretty much knew what to do. Set your feet, grip the ball, step forward, cock your arm back and release. So I did just that.

Right when I let go of the ball I knew that I'd thrown it pretty hard, so that was good. What I didn't know was that my pitch was five feet higher than my target. The softball left my hand and continued to rise well above Coach's head.

"Whoops," I giggled, embarrassed in front of all my teammates.

Coach stood up, looked back at me and smiled. "Well, you can pitch, you just can't aim." He laughed at his own joke. "It'll take some practice, but I think you can do it, Selena." I figured Coach was just trying to be nice.

A moment later, he took off his sunglasses and spoke to the team. "Marisa, get some rest tonight, you're starting tomorrow." I breathed a sigh of relief, glad that Coach wasn't thinking about me as a pitcher anymore. Just as I finished this thought he turned to me, "Selena, you'll start at first base, but be ready. You're gonna come in and relieve Marisa when she needs you."

I reacted confidently by nodding. I loved challenges, but what had I gotten myself into? Coach had seen that first pitch. It wasn't even close to his mitt, let alone being near the strike zone. I was definitely going to embarrass myself tomorrow.

That night, I didn't tell Mom or Dad about my pitching opportunity. I wanted to surprise them. But I did warn them not to miss tomorrow's game. When I got into bed that night my mind raced. I couldn't stop thinking about my new assignment. *What if I can't throw a strike? What if I walk like ten batters in a row and Coach pulls me from the game and all my teammates stop liking me and—* I stopped myself in the middle of these negative thoughts. I flipped the light switch on and sat upright in my favorite chair. Then I turned on the radio, listening to the last inning of the Arizona Scorpions game.

I was definitely one of the biggest Scorpion fans alive. Although I gave up playing baseball, I was still in love with the sport. I watched or listened to nearly every Scorpions game. I even sent letters to some of my favorite players—like Valentine, Rucker, Reyes and Kraft. Baseball still had an important role on the Field, too. My brother Carlos and I spent hours living out our fantasy baseball adventures there. He would crouch down like a catcher, and he'd relay the pitch sign between his legs. Then I'd windup and hurl the overhand pitch to the invisible batter.

Carlos couldn't help giving me a hard time about my new softball career. He would constantly throw the ball to me underhand and pretend to scream in a girlish voice. Sometimes I would get defensive. "Just because I play softball doesn't mean I'm not tough, Carlos. We play just as hard as the boys do." Although I believed this statement, my brother's jokes got to me sometimes.

The truth was, softball was becoming a bigger and bigger part of my life. Every day on the softball field I gained more friends. I became more of a leader in the lineup, too. Nobody was happier about all of this than Mom. Recognizing my boy-dominated neighborhood, she had always wanted me to connect with some girls. Seeing me bring home a softball teammate or go to a slumber party really thrilled her.

Mom was easy to spot when she was in the stands at my games. She always sat in her lawn chair up against the backstop. Everyone heard her clearly, as she shook a rock-filled soda can. She'd yell and scream and cheer, jumping up and down with every play. It was great, but really embarrassing at the same time. During my at-bats she was twice as loud. "Hit it out of the park, Selena! You can do it!" she'd scream.

The next day was the game I was slated to pitch in. Mom was in her chair directly behind home plate. I could hear her all the way from first base. In the top of the seventh, Coach told me to take the mound. We were leading 9-5. This was a great chance for me to get some game experience. In youth softball we only played seven innings. All I had to do was get three outs before our opponent scored four times and we'd win.

After tossing my final warm-up pitch, our short-stop, Anne, hollered, "Eat 'em up, Superestrella Cinderella!" I got that nickname, which means *Cinderella Superstar* in Spanish, from the fancy bows I wore. Mom's ribbons and bows made me feel like I was different than everyone else. They made me feel like I had something nobody else did.

A moment later, I turned toward the plate to start the inning. I had a straight-on view of my parents. Dad sat on the edge of the bench beside Mom in her lawn chair. I took a deep breath before tossing my first pitch high and wide. It hit the backstop with a clank, and I forced a smile. "That's alright!" Mom hollered and shook her can loudly. "Just relax. You can do it!"

Struggling with my footing on the mound, my

second pitch landed in the dirt. Ball two. Now I was sweating a bit. The body language of my teammates started to change too. I noticed Lisa Simpson holding her hands on her knees. Our outfielders were staring into space. Our catcher, Elizabeth Lee, was punching the center of her mitt nervously. My lack of confidence on the mound was spreading like a fire. The pressure really mounted when I tossed a third straight ball.

Fueled by frustration, my fourth pitch nearly hit the batter. I kicked the dirt as she walked toward first base. The girls in the opposing dugout began cheering louder. I could barely hear the shaking of Mom's can at this point. Elizabeth called time and jogged to the mound. "You didn't hit her, so that was good." She needled me with her dry sense of humor. This forced me to laugh and loosen up my shoulders. "You're fine, Selena. Just focus on my glove. You can do this." I shook my head slowly, barely listening. Elizabeth could tell she wasn't getting through to me. "Do you want to give up, Selena? Coach can always put Jessica in and—"

My eyes met Elizabeth's and she stopped talking. She knew I couldn't turn down a challenge. I spoke with force behind my words. "Keep Jessica in left field. Put your glove up and I'll hit it."

Elizabeth smiled. "Now that's better."

As the next batter dug in, I concentrated only on Elizabeth's mitt. I ignored Mom and Dad's cheers, my nervous teammates, my noisy opponents, and the hot Arizona sun. I set my feet, gripped the ball, and released the next pitch in one smooth motion. My hand's natural follow through landed my pitch in the heart of the leather glove. Pop! Strike one! *How did I do that?* I wondered.

Elizabeth flipped off her mask and smiled at me. I couldn't wait to get the ball back. I stared at the target again and my next pitch sailed right on line. Pop! Strike two! Now I was getting into a rhythm. I tossed another perfect pitch—right down the middle of the plate. This one may have been too perfect. The batter ripped it right back at me. Reacting on instinct, I threw my glove in front of my face and snatched the bullet.

"One out!" I yelled, holding up my pointer finger for everyone to see.

I started off the next batter with another down-the-middle pitch. This one was smacked into the left-centerfield gap for a double. The runner I'd walked scored from first. Knowing we still led 9-6 kept me pretty calm. I'd been finding the strike zone, and that was a positive. Now I needed to start moving the ball around the plate. I motioned for Elizabeth to visit the mound again.

When she reached me, I placed my glove over my mouth. I was trying to hide my words from my opponents. "Start moving your glove toward the corners. I think I can hit some different spots."

Elizabeth smacked me on the back with her

glove. "You got it!"

On the next pitch, Elizabeth placed her glove on the inside part of the plate. I hit the corner for strike one. After that toss I was officially in love with pitching. I tried not to get too excited on the mound. But the truth was I knew something important had just happened to me—I'd found my calling.

I aimed for the outside corner on the next pitch but missed by a few inches. So Elizabeth switched back to the inside part of the plate. Again, I was on target. Only this time the batter made contact. The ball bounced weakly off the handle of the bat. Our third baseman, Laura Simpson, ran toward the plate for the barehanded play. She scooped the ball cleanly, but her throw sailed wide down the first-base line. The runner from second scored on the play, cutting our lead to 9-7.

My inside pitch had jammed the batter perfectly. Her slow roller to third should have been an out. Instead, our lead was cut to two. Negative thoughts began to spin around in my head. *How could Laura miss that one? If she would have*—I stopped myself, realizing how unfair I was being. I'd made plenty of errors in the field before. I couldn't blame my teammates. I had to move on. It didn't matter that I'd done everything right.

I took a deep breath and pulled my cap down on my head. Hillary Jax, a friend of mine from school, was up at the plate. She was a tall, muscular girl with a huge uppercut swing. I'd watched her crush a double earlier in the game. With one out and a runner on second, Hillary lined up close to home plate. Reality started to set in: we'd outplayed this team the entire game and I was about to blow it.

I took another deep breath. Using a stronger leg push off the rubber, I threw my fastest pitch of the day. Hillary was surprised and had a hard time catching up with it. She bounced one softly to second base for out number two. *That was a good pitch*, I thought.

One more out and I could actually call today a success. With a runner on second, the cleanup hitter came to the plate. She glared at me confidently. My first three pitches were low and hard, producing a 2-1 count. The next pitch elevated coming off my hand. It reached the batter right about chest high. She took a hefty swing at this one, sending the ball high to short left field. I pointed up in the air immediately as I watched the ball soar toward Jessica McDonald. She ran under it and seemed to have it tracked. I sighed with relief, knowing that the game was about to be over. But as the ball came down, Jessica lost it in the bright sun. It dropped in front of her untouched. The runner from second base scored and our lead was cut to just one run.

I tugged on my visor again as I headed back to the mound. My stomach muscles tightened. My hands were shaking. Sweat was dripping down my back. I could hear my heart beating over the loud shaking of

Mom's soda can. My toes settled on the rubber and I zoned in on the plate. Elizabeth pounded her glove. "Right here, Selena!"

My first pitch hit the outside corner for strike one. That was exactly where I'd aimed that one. Feeling confident, I tried the same spot again, but missed low. That pitch evened the count at one-and-one. Elizabeth slid inside on the next pitch. With a smooth windmill rotation I connected with her glove. Pop! Strike two! The crowd stood on their feet. I was pumped up by the moment—maybe too pumped. Before I knew it, I'd thrown two straight pitches out of the strike zone. The count was full, three balls and two strikes. There was a runner on second with two outs, our team leading 9-8. This was a big pitch.

Elizabeth positioned her glove a bit inside again. As I released the ball, it headed in that direction. The batter swung quickly and smashed a line drive. If it stayed fair, the game would be tied. *Go foul, go foul, go foul.* I leaned toward the line, trying to urge the ball. "Foul ball," the umpire shouted, as the ball landed just outside the foul line.

I turned my back to the plate and smiled in relief at my teammates. Our shortstop, Anne Fishburn, smiled back at me. "Finish her off Superestrella Cinderella!" she shouted.

Just then, an idea entered my head. The batter was swinging out in front of my pitches. It was the perfect time to throw my very first changeup. A changeup is thrown with less speed than a fastball. I'd never thrown one before, but I knew I was supposed to bury the ball in the palm of my hand. With small hands and even smaller fingers, I found this grip to be no easy task. Still, I was willing to risk everything on this next pitch.

I stretched my fingers and palm around the ball. I concentrated on Elizabeth's glove. *Focus, Selena.* I then repeated the same windmill motion that had become natural for me that day. As my hand released the ball, I watched it float in slow motion toward home plate. Everyone was surprised by my trick pitch, particularly the batter. She had timed her swing for a fastball. Her huge cut was way out in front of my final pitch. The ball landed softly in the middle of Elizabeth's glove and the umpire shouted—"Strike three! That's the ballgame!"

I pounded my fist into my glove in excitement. I did it! It wasn't pretty, but we'd won the game. My teammates rushed around me. Coach Shepard joined our celebration. "Looks like we've got a new pitcher, girls!" he smiled.

I felt like I was glowing as I soaked up the amazing moment—I was a pitcher. With one huge save under my belt, life couldn't have been better.

CHAPTER FOUR

A GOODNIGHT KISS

"Come on guys, dinner's ready!" Mom yelled from the kitchen. The boys turned off their video games and Dad stopped reading his magazine. They all raced down the hallway. I finished helping Mom set the table by dropping three ice cubes into everyone's glass.

We'd returned home from the first softball game I'd ever pitched in an hour earlier. I was still floating from the excitement. I paced around the kitchen as Mom pulled one of her homemade specialties out of the oven. She was serving hot tamales with refried beans and rice. Mom cooked traditional Mexican food every chance she got. She thought it was important for us to stay close to our roots. She and Dad also spoke Spanish often.

We gathered around our old wood dining table,

eyeing the tamales and corn tortillas. The corners of the table had been chewed up by Campeóna. Mom kept them hidden by a bright yellow tablecloth she'd sewn herself two summers ago. We couldn't afford to buy a new table after Campeóna had used the corners as a chew toy. Instead, Mom bought some fabric and went to work. That was a perfect example of her tremendous spirit.

"When you get lemons, you make lemonade." Mom would always use that expression. Doing the best you could with what you were given was important to Mom. She had a way of making the darkness turn to light.

Everyone sat down in their regular seats and dug in. As usual, I sat between Joe and Carlos. Dad started this custom a few years earlier in order to separate the boys. They were always poking or kicking one another under the table. It wasn't uncommon for me to receive an occasional shoe to the shin during a meal. Not today, though. When hot tamales were on the table, the boys were silent—aside from the occasional request for more salsa.

"So boys, did you hear about Selena's game?" Mom spoke to my brothers. Their focus was barely interrupted as they piled refried beans into their tortillas.

"Yeah, Dad told us about it," said Joe.

"She was awesome!" Dad echoed Mom's excitement.

"How awesome can you be at *soft*ball?" Joe laughed, accenting the word soft.

My heart sank for a moment. Joe saw that his comment hurt my feelings and changed his tone. "I'm only kidding, Selena. I know how good you are."

"Only one batter really hit the ball hard and I caught it, Joe." My focus quickly turned away from Joe and toward Carlos. "Carlos, remember how you told me about the first time you pitched? You said that you loved being in control of the game. Remember? Well, it was just like that for me. I loved being on the mound. I know my teammates helped me, but I threw strikes. I had to look all those batters right in the eyes before I threw a pitch to them." I smiled, and then showed the boys exactly how I stared down the hitters.

Dad nudged Joe. "Your sister is really something, Jose." Dad always came to my rescue when it came to my brothers. I was his baby girl and he was protective of me. Dinner went on like that for the next fifteen minutes or so. I recapped nearly every pitch I threw. Mom smiled, Dad nodded, and my brothers gobbled tamale after tamale.

I jumped into a hot shower right after dinner. I was unable to get the feeling of excitement out of my head. The spraying water drowned out all the other sounds in the house. I started to daydream about pitching in middle school, in high school, in college, in the Olympics— "Hurry up, Selena!" My daydream ended quickly as Carlos pounded on the locked door.

Ten minutes later, after drying off, I ran over to Mom. She was exhausted, lying on her bed with her eyes closed. Dad and the boys were watching television. I laid down next to her. She sighed and closed her eyes, gently running her fingers through my hair. "What do you think about curls for tomorrow's dance?" Tomorrow was the annual father-daughter dance at my school, La Presa Elementary.

"Sure," I answered. "If you're tired, though, I can just—"

"Shhhhh," she sat up and began combing out my hair. Mom worked quickly, humming softly as she placed my hair in curlers. When she'd finished, I rushed toward the mirror to look at myself. Then I lied down on Mom's bed to test them, checking if I would be able to sleep. The discomfort caused me to sit up. "How do I sleep like this?" I asked.

Mom shrugged her shoulders. "You'll manage."

Sometimes I felt really unlucky to be a girl. I mean, it was so easy for boys. Especially when it came to sports. Because I was a girl, everyone expected me to prefer dolls to baseball gloves. I didn't, though. Sure, I liked to wear nice clothes. But compared to getting ready to play ball, being girly was a lot of work. I touched the rollers on my head again as I sneaked a peek in the living room. My lazy brothers were sprawled out on our old tan couch, which doubled as my bed. "Oh well," I sighed. "I won't sleep much, but at least

I'll look pretty for the dance."

Mom laughed at this comment. "You will too sleep. It just feels funny at first."

"It feels like I have a pile of bricks sticking into the back of my head. How am I supposed to sleep with a brick head?"

Mom laughed. "You can use my special pillow tonight, Selena. That should help with the bricks." She left the room. When she returned a minute later she was holding a shiny, rose colored dress. She was also carrying her pillow. "I ironed your dress," she handed it to me and I thanked her. Then she handed me the pillow. "I want this back tomorrow night." She tossed the pillow to me. As she followed through with the throwing motion, she looked like she was in pain.

"Are you alright Mom?" I placed the pillow back on the bed.

"Just a little heartburn from dinner. I'm fine. I'm glad you're out there pitching and not me." Mom sat down as I tried on my dress for her. I did an imitation of a ballerina, prancing in circles around the room. My curlers were bouncing all over the place. I even tried spinning on my toe, but tripped. I had never been graceful. Mom stood up and we laughed as she twirled me around like her dance partner.

Knowing it was late, we walked to the couch, which also served as my bed. "Okay boys, off your sister's bed." She smacked my brothers playfully on the backs of their heads. Joe and Carlos scattered into their shared bedroom after kissing Mom on the cheek. Then Mom laid me down, wrapping my blanket around me. "What a great day." Her smile was big and bright.

I answered back, "Yeah, I think I'm gonna always pitch from now on—if they let me."

Mom smiled. "They'll let you. You see, things never work out the way you plan them. If you give them the chance though, they work out all the same. You were great today, and you really seemed to love it out there."

"I did." I smiled thinking about the feeling I had on the mound that day. I had found my calling. "I love you, Mom."

"I love you too, sweetheart." She kissed me on the forehead and shut the lamp off near my head. Staring at me with her warm, brown eyes, she paused before kissing me on the forehead again. "Sweet dreams."

I slept soundly that night, dreaming of stepping onto that pitcher's mound again.

The next morning I awoke early to the horrible sound of weeping.

My entire life changed that day. I ripped off my blankets the second I heard the crying. I ran down the hall as fast as I could. When I reached my parents' bedroom, I found Dad sitting on his bed. He was crying. Mom's body lay limp in his arms.

I stood in the doorway with my brothers behind me, frozen in shock. Tears welled up in my eyes as I waited for Mom to wake up. Only she never did. I had never seen my Dad look so sad or scared. Nothing could have prepared me for the loss of my mother. When Maria Nora Garcia passed away in her sleep, I was changed forever.

I couldn't stop staring at the casket during my mother's funeral. I held her prayer card in my hand tightly—there was a simple picture of her on it. It brought back a rush of happy memories. I thought of her can-shaking cheers at my softball games, her warm smile and her loud laugh. Then I remembered our final moments together—dancing, laughing and then kissing each other goodnight.

I didn't hear anything that was said at the funeral. I didn't feel any of the hugs or handshakes. I felt numb, lifeless, dried up, empty. Like a fish in the desert. I missed fifth grade graduation and all the festivities that went with it—including the father-daughter dance. I didn't care about any of that stuff with Mom gone. In fact, I wondered if I would ever want to dance again. My eleventh birthday was the quietest of my life. I didn't even eat a piece of the cake Dad bought for me. I quit playing softball too. I spent most of my summer days crying.

Three months later, even the novelty of entering middle school didn't excite me. With Mom gone, I didn't know what I wanted to do with my life. Nothing seemed important to me anymore.

CHAPTER FIVE

A CHALLENGE

Middle school started and it was horrible. In the year after Mom's death, I rarely left our apartment. The only people I spoke to were my brothers and my Dad. It seemed like no one understood the pain I felt. Joe and Carlos never really talked about serious stuff, so I was on my own with my feelings. Sure, they experienced the same loss I did, but somehow it was different. They seemed to be able to go on with their lives. I found it hard to breathe some days.

Carlos and I walked through the front door after school together every day. Right away, he would drop his backpack and head to the Field. All his problems disappeared down there. I was always invited, but I had no interest in going. I quit playing all sports after Mom's death. I did still watch the Scorpions play on television, though. It was one of the few things Dad and I did together. Aside from television, I was completely disconnected with baseball and softball.

But near the end of sixth grade, something amazing happened to me. And it helped me out of my depression. It all started when Carlos and I dropped by the school library. As we walked past the librarian, we noticed a poster for a "Readathon Challenge." A picture of Arizona Scorpions home run-hitting king, Jose Valentine, was attached to the side.

I didn't read the details, but Carlos sure did. He caught up to me in the back of the library. Playfully slapping me on the shoulder, Carlos spoke in a loud whisper: "Hey, Selena, did you see that Readathon sign? Did you see the prizes?"

He held a yellow flyer in his hand. I looked up as he ran his finger straight down to the prize category. He read aloud: "There are first, second, and third place prizes for each grade level. Plus, a grand prize!" His eyes opened wide as he spoke. "The grand prize—for the kid who reads the most books in the entire school—is two tickets to a Scorpions game PLUS a personal tour of Arizona Stadium." I raised my head from my book as Carlos slapped my back. "Can you imagine, Selena?"

I tried to pretend I wasn't interested. "Thanks Carlos, but no thanks."

"Come on, Selena!" Carlos wouldn't give up. "Imagine being on the field with Jose Valentine and

Tony Rocker. Would that be awesome or what?"

I quickly put my hand over his mouth, trying to muffle his excitement. "Shhh, we're in the library."

Carlos lowered his voice. "Well, I bet I can read more books than you can, anyway."

He knew that I hated turning down a challenge. I had changed since Mom's death, though. "That doesn't work on me anymore, Carlos."

He paused for a second as I flipped through a book. For some reason, he desperately wanted me to enter this contest. I wasn't budging. That is, until he said something that really got my blood boiling. "What would Mom think of the way you're acting, Selena?"

His words echoed in my ears. I nearly dropped the book I was flipping through. The truth was, I knew exactly what Mom would think. She would want me to stop feeling sorry for myself. She'd want me to improve my grades and rejoin the softball team. Most of all, she'd want me to bring the smile back to my face. Although I knew this, it was hard to accept. "Mom is dead, Carlos," I replied coldly to his comment and walked away, near tears.

Immediately, my brother grabbed me by the arm and spoke forcefully. "Wait a minute! I loved Mom too, Selena. *I* still remember how she wanted us to do great things. Maybe you forgot." He paused, his tone softening, "Do you remember what she used to say to us? When you get lemons—"

"You make lemonade," I finished his sentence

and our eyes met. A tear ran down my cheek.

Carlos gave me a hug and I started to cry. "You're right. I'll do it Carlos." We reached out our right hands and knocked fists, sealing the pact.

Ten minutes later I had loaded five sports books into my arms and was excited to begin. I picked up a fictional story about a baseball player heading for the majors. Then I grabbed an instructional softball book that focused on pitching. I also picked up a few basketball books and a football book too.

For the next four weeks, all I did was read. My log sheet was jammed from top to bottom with the thirty-four books I'd read! I smiled confidently as I handed off the stack of papers to the librarian. My sidekick, Carlos, who was competing for the eighth grade, did the same. His thirteen-book effort came up well short of mine, though.

I was excited when Carlos and I sat down in the school auditorium the next afternoon. Our principal held a sheet of paper in her hand at the podium. I nervously rubbed my thumbs together as I waited for her make the announcements. I slid to the edge of my seat. Sixth grade was going to be the first class to receive awards. Before I knew it, she said: "The winner for sixth grade is Selena Garcia!"

I started tapping my feet in excitement and relief. Winning my grade guaranteed me two tickets to a Scorpions game. Now the real question came up: was I the best in the school? That's what counted—that's what would get me the tour of the stadium. I held in my emotions, realizing that both seventh and eighth grade still needed to be announced. "The first-place winner for seventh grade is Nathan Jaybee!" Only one more grade to go. "And the first-place winner for eighth grade is Hannah Mendoza! Congratulations to all the winners. Now, for the grand prize." My heart leaped in my chest. "The grand prize winner for all of Highlands Middle School is Selena Garcia, with thirty-four books!"

Cheers and claps surrounded me as I jumped up from my seat. My feet shuffled at the pace of a home run trot—fast enough to admit excitement, but slow enough to appreciate the moment. When I returned to my seat I was holding an envelope. Inside, were two "all-access" tickets. I gave my brother a big hug. "We're going, man! We're gonna see the Scorpions up close and personal!" I looked toward the ceiling and wondered if Mom was watching. I was sure that she'd be proud if she was. For the first time since her death, I felt my heart thump with excitement. I actually had something to smile about.

The Scorpions game was a month later. I couldn't have been more excited. We jumped into Dad's pickup and headed to the ballpark right after school. The drive took about two hours, but the time flew by. When we reached the Scorpion Way exit, Dad even became excited. "There it is guys!" He pointed to Arizona Stadium on the right-hand side of the car. Carlos and I slid over to the window.

"No way!" I turned and knuckle bumped Carlos.

After we parked, Dad purchased a ticket for himself. Carlos and I entered the stadium with the two free tickets I had won. Our seats were in a great spot, right above the Scorpions dugout. After checking me into the public relations office, Dad and Carlos found their seats.

An older woman with thick-rim glasses offered her right hand to me. "I'm Pat Rogers, I'll be giving you the tour of the stadium." We shook hands and I smiled. Then I joined the group of kids who had won this honor for their school, and we began the tour. The eight boys and four girls shuffled into an elevator after showing a security guard our passes. As we started going down toward the locker-room, my heart pounded. When the elevator doors opened I realized where I was—beneath the stadium. This was a place I'd never dreamed of seeing in person.

We approached the locker-room and my senses heightened. My ears perked up at the sound of music playing. When we entered the room, I noticed four speakers hanging in the corners. Strolling by the lockers, my eyes widened. I read the names on the gold plaques: #31 Jose Valentine, #19 Tony Rocker, #14 Dan Foote, #51 Trevor Kraft. Bright white jerseys with players' names sewn in blue letters hung in each locker. Gloves, boxes of cleats and dozens of bats filled the open spaces. I reached down and touched the carpet without anyone noticing. There was no doubt that this was the coolest room I had ever seen.

We headed out of the clubhouse and I turned around for one last glimpse. Then I followed the group down a long tunnel. It was dimly lit and shaped like an upside-down U. The walls were covered with photographs. As I moved toward the end of the hallway, a light shone in the distance. Within a few seconds I was staring at the openness of a professional baseball field. The massive concrete ring of the stadium cradled the green grass. Banks of lights shone down on the red brick clay. I took my first steps onto the field and felt so excited I almost screamed. My eyes were wider than ever before.

I was out of my trance a moment later. I could hear the sound of wood connecting with the leather of a tightly wound baseball. My attention quickly turned toward the batting cage. "Crack!" "Crack!" "Crack!" The Scorpions had just begun batting practice. I sat down on the bench inside the dugout. *This is so cool,* I thought.

Just then I noticed Jose Valentine stepping to the plate. I quickly walked over to the grass, admiring his thick muscles. His quick bat speed produced a line drive into the gap and a few blasts over the outfield wall. Several other Scorpions took their turns in the batting cage. Groups of position players moved from fielding, to running the bases, to batting. Most of the pitchers ran and stretched in the outfield. The pregame warm-up worked like the inside of a clock— one gear moving another gear, which moved another gear.

Nothing stunned me more than the size of the 6-foot-5-inch, 250-pound Valentine. I stared in awe as he walked over to our group. "How you guys doing?" He stuck out his gigantic hand to each of us.

I smiled as my tiny hand was swallowed up by his enormous grip. Valentine grabbed his dark brown bat and held it across his chest. "I hear you guys are great readers. Well, I've got another contest for you. I'm going to pick a number between one and one hundred. Whoever gets closest can have this bat *and* my batting gloves."

Number thirty-one immediately flashed into my mind. That was Valentine's jersey number. I could only hope the students in front of me would avoid my number. Valentine stared at the sky, thinking of his pick. Then he lowered his head. "Okay, I got it. We'll start right here." He pointed to the girl who stood in front of me.

"Fourteen," she responded. The rest of the kids followed. "Fifty, sixty-one, twenty-three, seventy-nine, forty-two, eight." When it was my turn I looked into Valentine's eyes and confidently declared, "Thirty-one."

After the rest of the kids had guessed their numbers, Valentine lifted up the giant bat. "And the winner is," he paused to add some drama, "number," then he pointed to his jersey, "thirty-one!" I moved toward Valentine, my excitement pushing me forward.

Valentine pulled me aside and handed me his batting gloves and bat. Then he sat down next to me in the dugout. "So, do you play ball?"

I looked away. "Yeah, I used to play softball."

"Used to?" he asked. "You retired already?" He laughed at his own joke.

"No." I forced a smile. "My Mom died a year ago, so I quit playing." I tried hard not to cry as I spoke those words to my hero.

Valentine rested his hand on my shoulder. "I'm sorry to hear that." Wanting to break the silence, he continued. "Did she come to a lot of your games?"

"Every single one." I answered.

"Wow, she must have loved watching you, huh?"

"Yeah," I spoke through a tight smile. "I loved it, too. Especially pitching, but I only got to pitch once." Tears welled up in my eyes again as I began to remember that long day—the day that I fell in love with pitching and lost my best friend.

"I bet you were pretty good with those big biceps of yours." Valentine jokingly squeezed my arm muscles. It made me laugh as I wiped a tear from my eye. He continued, "I know it's none of my business, but I think your mom would want you to keep playing. Don't you?"

I shyly nodded. "Yeah, that's what everyone keeps telling me."

"Maybe they're right. Do you think you can find your mitt and get back on a team? You already got some new batting gloves." He paused, waiting for my response. As I shrugged my shoulders, he continued. "I don't know you, but you got here, somehow. And that took heart. I believe that you have the heart to get back on the field too."

"Thank you, Jose." In that moment, everything stopped. I was sitting in the dugout in Arizona Stadium chatting with Jose Valentine. Talk about a strange moment. All of a sudden I started to smile as I spoke: "I think you're right, Jose, I really *should* play again."

Valentine offered his hand and we shook on the deal. When we released our grip, I felt as if a weight had been lifted off my shoulders. Jose made his way back to his teammates and I made my way into the stands.

I told Dad and Carlos about my deal with Jose Valentine. As soon as we got back home, I would start my softball career again. I was determined to not only return, but to come back as a pitcher. During the seventh-inning stretch, I paused to soak in my first great day in a long time. Although I still thought about Mom all the time, I could feel myself changing. The hard shell I'd been carrying in my mother's absence was beginning to crack. I was finally ready to open my wings again and revisit the world of softball.

CHAPTER SIX

NOBODY'S PERFECT

Making my comeback as a softball pitcher was extra tough because I had no catcher. My brothers were hardly ever around so I had to be creative. Within a few weeks, I discovered the perfect partner just a twenty-minute walk from our apartment: the old racquetball court at Highlands Middle School.

I made the trip every day. I'd bring five softballs, a bottle of water, my glove, and two pieces of white chalk. A concrete wall intended for racquetball stood about twenty feet high in the middle of the blacktop area. I would draw a square strike zone in the middle of the cement structure. Beside the box would be a stick-figure batter. I'd use my chalk to mark a pitching mound. Then I'd fire away, windmilling pitch, after pitch, after pitch.

Without any distractions I was able to concentrate on changing speeds, being consistent, and nailing the edges of the strike zone. My control improved steadily. To my surprise, I also noticed an increase in my pitch speed. My right arm grew stronger and stronger from the practice. In addition to pitching, I spent time tossing up balls and hitting them at the wall. Swinging that bat felt great. After an hour of exercise, I wanted more than anything to play in a game.

Two months after I began my training, I was finally ready for the real thing. I could hardly sit still on the drive over to that first practice. I was really nervous about seeing all my teammates again. *What if they didn't want me back? What if they were upset that I'd quit?* These thoughts quickly disappeared. The girls greeted me with excited hugs in the parking lot right when Dad dropped me off. *What a relief!*

On the field, I had very little trouble. I slipped right back into the routine. Everyone knew me as a good fielder and hitter, so they weren't too surprised. When I hopped onto the mound, though, my powerful pitching shocked them. Throwing to Elizabeth was much easier than throwing at a wall. I found myself pitching better than ever. I threw about ten fastballs in a row that smacked the center of Elizabeth's glove. My teammates circled around me—their mouths hanging open in shock.

My heart jumped when I put on my Orange Crush uniform again. When it was time for my first game back, Coach Larry really shocked me—he told me that I was the starting pitcher. Before stepping onto the mound, I reached into the back pocket of my shorts. I had placed Mom's prayer card there. I rubbed my fingers on it for luck. I vowed to place the photograph there during every game I ever played. Even though I couldn't see Mom in her lawn chair, I kept her spirit alive in my back pocket. The only uncomfortable feeling I experienced that day came from my hair. Without Mom's ponytails and braids, my long black hair blew freely in the breeze.

I anchored my cleats on the freshly dusted rubber. It was then when I started to notice something. I felt different today. My mind was completely focused on pitching this game. It was as if *this* game was the only thing happening in the entire world. I began to notice things I'd never seen before. The curves and creases on Elizabeth's mitt became clear. I could even see her fingers moving behind the thick leather. She was adjusting her target to an exact spot. And I knew I could hit it.

After a deep breath and a final glance at the hitter, I twirled my arm forward. The ball zipped out of my hand and snapped the center of Elizabeth's glove. Strike one. The Orange Crush fans erupted in excitement, especially Dad. My next two pitches were similar to the first. The Blue Bombers leadoff batter was stunned. She stood motionless as the umpire rung her up for the first out of the game. My heart beat excitedly with my first chance success.

The second Blue Bombers batter dug in and swung at my first offering. She weakly grounded the outside pitch to second base. Meredith Manning scooped this one up and ran it over to first. I eased up the speed a bit to the next batter. Unfortunately, my changeup didn't trick her. She pulled a laser down the left-field line. Our left fielder, Laura Simpson, was on her toes and snagged the sizzling shot for the third out. A sense of relief rushed over me like a warm shower.

We hustled into the dugout and I smiled from ear to ear. I had passed my first test. I'd made it through one inning without giving up a hit. But before I could even pump my fist, I was grabbing a batting helmet. I hit third in the lineup, which meant that I had to get ready in a hurry. I wore my Jose Valentine batting gloves, even though they were big on me. I just had to.

I stepped up to the plate with the bases empty and two outs. The first two pitches missed the strike zone. With a 2-0 count in my favor, I guessed that the next pitch would be a strike. Sure enough, I was right. The fastball came right down the middle and I pulled the trigger. I took all of my frustration out on that swing. I hadn't played softball for nearly two years! Being back—and swinging at a 2-0 fastball meant everything to me. My bat hit the ball with a solid crack. Their left fielder chased after it, deep down the line. The ball continued to sail as if being propelled by an engine. When it finally landed, it rolled through the endless outfield.

Meanwhile, I was sprinting toward second base. As I raced toward third I was sure I'd be safe. So was Coach Larry. He was so sure, that he was still waving as I made my way toward the bag. His arms signaled for me to keep my head down and keep running. He was sending me home! I pounced my foot on the third base bag and shoved off toward the plate.

From the corner of my eye, I watched their shortstop take the cutoff throw from left field. She spun around and fired one toward the plate. Her throw was off-target and I didn't even have to slide. I was easily safe at home. My home run had the scoreboard reading: Orange Crush 1, Blue Bombers 0.

We kept our lead through the first five innings, adding on three more runs. But the story of the day was happening on the pitcher's mound. Somehow, I had sailed through the first five innings without allowing one single hit. Although this was incredible, my main focus was still winning the game. I only hoped my stamina would carry me through to the finish line.

I started to get tired in the top of the sixth. I walked the leadoff batter after throwing some awful pitches. She advanced to second on a ground out and then to third on a sacrifice bunt. Luckily, she never made it home. I got out of the inning with a fastball that their number nine hitter couldn't catch up to.

I clenched my fist in excitement as I entered the

dugout for the final inning. All I needed were three more outs to collect a no-hitter. *Stay calm,* I thought, *stop thinking so much. Just keep pitching,* I told myself. Ten agonizing minutes later, we made our third out. I hustled to the mound with a 6-0 lead.

With a no-hitter on the line, I thought hard about each pitch I threw. The truth was, I didn't know very much about pitching. Most of what I had done so far had been based on instinct. What I did know was that throwing early strikes had been the key to my success all day. So I made sure to groove the first pitch of the inning right down the middle. On the next pitch, I went for the inside corner. The hitter stood frozen, strike two.

Although I never received any pitching training, I had watched a ton of baseball games. So I knew that with an 0-2 count I could afford to waste a pitch. This meant that even if I threw a ball, I would still be ahead of the hitter. I considered tossing one out of the strike zone. My hope being that the batter would swing at a bad pitch. Then I considered my tired right arm. I decided that instead of wasting energy, I would try for the outside corner. My pitch sailed a little high. The hitter clubbed a liner that looped into the glove of our first baseman, Clara Perez. That was an easy first out.

"Good pitch, Selena." Elizabeth shouted from behind the plate.

I wiped a pool of sweat from my forehead. "One out!" I shouted to my teammates. I held my pointer finger high in the air. Wanting to maintain my focus, I zeroed in on home plate. It was difficult to avoid all the distractions. There was chatter in our opponent's dugout. Plus, the excited crowd cheering me on was loud and intimidating. Sweat dripped off every part of my body.

The first two pitches I threw to the next batter resulted in a 1-1 count. The third pitch rolled off my fingertips oddly. The ball hopped toward the back-stop. *What was that?* I wondered. On the fourth pitch, I thought I caught the outside corner for strike two, but the umpire disagreed. The count was now 3-1—a hitter's count. I definitely didn't want to give in with a "meat" pitch, so I went low and outside.

The pitch was perfect and the batter dribbled one toward second. Meredith Manning fielded it cleanly, but lost her footing while making the toss to first. The ball flew into our dugout and the runner advanced to second. Meredith dropped her head in disappointment. I turned toward her. "Don't worry about it, Mer." I said these words aloud, but inside I was frustrated.

Although my no-hitter was still intact, I wasn't sure if I had anything left in my pitching arm. I pulled my visor down over my closed eyes and pictured a perfect strike. I flashed this picture in my mind over and over. Eventually, I forgot about Meredith, her error, the runner, and the crowd.

Moving toward the rubber I looked up at their number three batter. She was a power-hitting lefty who was crowding the plate. As the first pitch flew toward her, she squared around to bunt. The ball bounced off of her bat right in front of home plate and died. I knew there was no way I could reach it in time. *Oh no,* I thought, *you're gonna lose your no-hitter on a bunt!* Just as this thought went through my head, Elizabeth made an amazing play. She sprung out from behind home plate like a hungry cat and tossed a bullet to Clara at first. The runner was out by a thumbnail.

"Great play, Liz! Two outs!" Meredith shouted, holding up two fingers.

Elizabeth's play energized me and I ran back to the rubber with a skip in my step. I pointed at her, excitedly. Then I placed my glove to my heart. I could feel it pounding through my jersey top. My long hair was blowing in front of my face. I was one out away from a lifetime achievement. I toed the rubber and confidently stared into Elizabeth's glove.

My first offering zipped in and caught the inside corner, strike one. I barely took any time before unleashing my second pitch. This one popped as it hit Elizabeth's glove for strike two. The crowd stood. The runner at third base started running up and down the line. She was trying to break my concentration. I felt myself falling into the eye of a tornado. The crowd and the chatter on the field swirled around me. I needed to find my focus again. I knew exactly where to look. I slid my right hand into my back pocket. It was there that I felt the comfort of Mom's prayer card. I smiled thinking about her. Right away, the butterflies disappeared. The tornado was replaced by the quiet peace of the Arizona sun and Mom's presence on the mound with me.

I peered up at Elizabeth, who pounded her glove. "Right here, Selena! One more strike!"

I followed her orders, delivering a perfect pitch for a storybook-ending strike three. But unfortunately, this wasn't a storybook. The Blue Bombers batter swung and connected. I watched as the ball floated off her bat and sailed toward shallow left field. *Oh no*, I thought. The ball began to lose steam just out of the reach of Anne Fishburn. I held my mitt near my face as I watched the ball begin its descent. This one was definitely going to drop in.

Then, from out of nowhere, I noticed our left fielder, Shannon Edison. She was running at the ball with a full head of steam. She wasn't going to give up on this one. *Come on Shannon,* I thought. "Get there Shannon!" I screamed. Just then, Shannon dropped into a feet-first slide. I started running toward the plate to back up our catcher in case of a throw home. I backpedaled from the mound, never taking my eyes off of Shannon. She rolled over twice and then jumped to her feet—holding in her hand the red-laced softball!

Three outs! Game over! My no-hitter was complete!

I sprinted out to Shannon in left. The rest of

my teammates joined the celebration. We rolled around like lunatics, blades of grass sticking in our hair and teeth.

The buzz around the Bobby Sox community was all about my no-hitter. The word even reached the neighboring town of La Mira. At our third Orange Crush game of the season, a woman named Victoria Joyce approached me. Victoria was a former college softball pitcher who grew up in La Mira. She was kind of a legend in Arizona's softball community. She was just twenty-three years old, but already a respected coach. I guessed that she'd heard about my accomplishment from one of her players.

Mom always told me that things never work out the way you plan them—but if you have patience, they work out all the same. I never planned for Mom to leave. I never planned on being a pitcher. I certainly never planned on throwing a no-hitter. But these events brought a very special person into my life.

Victoria shook my hand with a loose grip. "Wow, congratulations on that no-hitter. I heard all about it." I smiled as she continued to speak. "You know, I teach lessons to some of the best pitchers around here. I was wondering if you would be interested."

"Me?" I asked, uncertain. "One of the best pitchers around?" I cracked a half-smile. "Really?"

"Sure. You definitely got everyone's attention

last week. I heard you were untouchable." Something drew me to Victoria immediately. She was in amazing physical shape for starters. Not an ounce of fat showed on her 5-foot-10-inch frame. Yet her rock-hard muscles did not match her soft and sweet personality. Her strength and sweetness represented the balance I was searching for in myself. After only talking with her for twenty seconds I knew that Victoria and Mom would have gotten along well. Of course, this made me like her even more. "What do you think, Selena?" Victoria asked.

"Well, I'll have to talk to my dad." I knew that lessons cost money, and that was going to be a problem. "He's right over there." I pointed to the gate down the right field fence. I waved Dad over and he joined us near the dugout.

The two of them shook hands. I twisted my long black hair around my finger, wondering if Victoria would be able to convince Dad. I let them talk for awhile, standing about ten feet away. I was just close enough to catch the gist of the conversation. Victoria jumped right in, giving Dad all the information. Dad seemed interested and kept saying, "That would be great." He explained that he loved my involvement with softball. Dad was also very honest, though, letting Victoria know that money was an obstacle.

For some reason, Dad seemed pretty comfortable with Victoria. The two of them talked in the dugout for over an hour. I tossed the ball around with

Anne Fishburn just a few feet away. I heard Dad sharing the story of Mom's death. Victoria listened compassionately. After speaking to Dad a little bit longer, she came up with an idea.

A moment later, they called me over. They had discussed a way for me to work off Victoria's coaching fee. She was an incredibly busy lady. Victoria worked every day as a student teacher. Plus, she coached games for a junior varsity team. Then, at night, she went to school to receive her teaching credentials. Her problem was that her dog, Sammy, was home alone all day long. She needed someone to walk him. As it turned out, Victoria had just moved to an apartment in Tierra de Sueño. Her place was three blocks from my house! She'd planned on hiring someone to walk the dog. Like Mom always said, plans hardly ever turn out the way you plan them.

I told Victoria how much I loved dogs and how happy I'd be to walk Sammy. So in a stroke of luck— we struck a deal.

Two days later, I arrived at my first session. Victoria showed me things I'd never even heard or thought of. She started with the basics, teaching me stretches to loosen up my pitching arm. Then she showed me the right way to position my toes on the pitching rubber. This was important. When done correctly, the toes point towards the target on take-off and the right foot drags behind. This allows for greater push-off and accuracy.

Most of the stuff Victoria talked about, I had been doing all wrong. This made sense. After all, I'd learned how to pitch by pitching. I was pretty good, too. But I'd never be able to reach my full potential without learning the right way to do it. In those first sixty minutes, Victoria taught me a ton. The skills we practiced never became boring. And she shared all kinds of stories with me. Each one related to the game in a different way. After just a few sessions, Victoria's mental approach to softball was rubbing off on me. I was starting to see the game differently. Under her instruction, I had adopted the mindset of a pitcher. And under my instruction, Sammy the dog was no longer peeing in Victoria's living room.

CHAPTER SEVEN

A BUMPY RIDE

That's how it went for me during the next six months. Victoria continued giving me pitching instruction, and I continued improving. I became very comfortable with my new coach. Our bond was so strong that I even began to share my thoughts about Mom's death. These were thoughts I'd never shared out loud. Talking about Mom really helped. The deep wounds I'd suffered were finally beginning to heal. Everything was working out—just like Mom said it would.

I remember one day of our training in particular. After a solid hour of drills, a heavy rain started pouring down. Now, where you live, this may be pretty common. Not in the Arizona desert, though. When it rains in Arizona you're never prepared. As the rain poured down in buckets, Victoria and I sat stranded in the dugout. We watched as the dusty infield dirt turned to dark brown mud. The rain splashed on the roof above us and Victoria shared a story with me. It was then I realized why Victoria had wanted to help me. Sure, the daily walk's I took Sammy on were a big help. But there was another reason she was so touched by my story. It turned out that we had a lot in common.

With tears trickling down her cheeks, Victoria explained how she too, had lost a parent. For her, it was her father, Phil. Like me, she'd had a difficult time getting back into life after that. That was why she decided to help me in the first place. She knew what I was going through from experience. I couldn't believe she'd waited six months to tell me that story. When she did, I felt closer to her than ever. She wiped the tears from her eyes and finished talking just as the rain stopped. Then we both stood up and made our way onto the muddy field. Victoria crouched down in the mud and I pitched to her. I knew somewhere, Maria and Phil were smiling.

Days like that meant the most to me. Still, the really fun stuff happened on game days. That was when I got to bring all my new skills to the pitcher's mound for the Orange Crush. By season's end, I had pitched in eight games and lost only once. More importantly, though, I'd learned how to pitch.

Under Victoria's watchful eye I became one of the top fourteen-and-under pitchers in Bobby Sox. I even began playing on a traveling team in the off season. Victoria was encouraging, too. She said that if I worked hard enough, softball would be my ticket to a free college education. With high school coming around the corner, I began to focus on that goal. I desperately wanted that scholarship. Any help I could give Dad financially was fine by me. Especially if all I had to do was pitch.

In high school softball, the games meant more than they did in Bobby Sox. There were section titles and playoff games to be won. Plus, it wasn't uncommon for college scouts to show up. Their job was to search for the best players. When they found them, they offered them scholarships to attend their schools. The question was: Would I be one of them?

A few months later, I was a high school freshman. I couldn't believe how fast time had traveled. It seemed like yesterday that I was ten, playing baseball with the boys. I was now fourteen years old! To be honest, high school wasn't as bad as I expected. Unlike middle school, I made new friends and adjusted quickly. The schoolwork was definitely tougher, though. There were a lot more tests and homework, too. Through hard work, I was able to maintain a high B average.

When spring came around I tried out for the varsity softball team. To my delight, Anne Fishburn and I both made it. We were the only freshmen who earned spots. The coach, Mrs. Moody, tagged me as the number two pitcher. I didn't mind the secondary role. Lulu Mendoza, our number one pitcher, had three years of varsity experience. Mrs. Moody, on the other hand, had no softball experience. Mrs. Moody taught physical education and knew a lot about fitness and health. Unfortunately, when it came to the ins and outs of softball—she didn't have a clue.

All the information Mrs. Moody got about softball came from a thick manual. She rolled it up and kept it with her at all times. It became a big joke. We even gave the book a title: "Softball for Dummies."

Mrs. Moody's philosophy was always "by the book." She never wavered from the text's suggestions. If a runner reached base with no outs, the next hitter always bunted—always. Why? Because the book said so. If the count was 3-0 on the cleanup hitter, we always walked her. Why? Because the book said so. This coaching style sucked the fun out of the game for all of us. Softball was not an exact science. Adjustments needed to be made on the fly. Risks needed to be taken! Surprises had to be thrown at an opponent in order to win.

At six-foot-two and close to two hundred pounds, Mrs. Moody was quite a presence. Her loud voice and mean expressions made her really intimidating. She also ran a very tight ship. If you were late for practice, you had to run wind sprints. If you missed a practice, you sat out a game. If you talked back, you sat out two games. This approach did not sit well with me. I preferred positive encouragement and pats on the back. After all, I was tough enough on myself. Mrs. Moody only added to my frustration.

The only good thing that happened in high school softball that year was that I made some friends. This helped to soften a rough season under the thumb of Coach Moody. Our games were about as fun as chewing on tinfoil. Our practices were ten times worse than that. In club, and Bobby Sox softball, under Coach Larry and Coach Wilson, I had a great time. We won a lot of games, too! Directed by Mrs. Moody, we failed in both of those departments.

With only five games left in the regular season, I blew up. Our team, the Monarchs, had won only four of the twenty games we'd played. But I was pumped to play our crosstown rivals anyway. The Del Ray Cougars had some great players. I started, and pitched solid through the first three innings of a scoreless tie. In the top of the fourth, however, the Cougars got to me.

It all started when their first batter of the inning bunted for a single. The next hitter, Kim McAnn, was the Cougars' feared cleanup batter. Monica Larson, my catcher, signaled for the rise ball. I shook my head, trying to get a new sign. I had played against Kim in club softball and knew she loved the high stuff. I also knew that Coach Moody never compromised. When Monica peered over to the dugout to get another sign, Moody wouldn't budge. The sign came in again— rise ball. I dug the ball deep into my glove and gripped my fingers along the seams.

I sighed deeply and threw the pitch, knowing it wouldn't be successful. I executed it to perfection. The ball rose out of my hand just as it was supposed to. Then it rose right off Kim's bat into center field. The speedy runner on first scored easily. Cougars 1, Monarchs 0. I shook my head in frustration. I knew these batters better than our coach, yet she demanded to be in control.

With Kim on second base, I struck out the next batter on pure fire. Next, the Cougars sent up Mercy Reyes. Strangely, she was batting left-handed, though she normally batted from the right side. I knew her plan right away. Mercy was going to slap a bunt down into the ground along the first-base line. Her slap bunt would be more effective from the left side. I knew if I kept the ball up, she wouldn't be able to pound the ball into the ground. I also had to keep the pitch outside so she couldn't leave the box early. That meant a rise ball on the outer part of the plate. I eyed Monica's fingers for the sign—drop ball. "Great call Mrs. Moody," I whispered under my breath. I bent down, faking like I needed to retie my laces. I couldn't believe Mrs. Moody! She had absolutely no understanding of pitch selection. *Why is she calling the shots, anyway?* I thought.

I flung my long hair away from my face and stepped off the mound. I hoped that Monica would flash a new sign. No such luck. I shook my head, letting her know that I did not agree with the pitch. Then I heard a booming voice from the dugout, "Quit shaking me off, Selena!" Mrs. Moody's shout made everyone aware of our power struggle. My face flashed red in embarrassment.

I didn't look at my angry coach as I slid my fingers over the ball and dug into the rubber. Frustrated, I tossed a bad pitch. The ball spun off my fingers and landed in the dirt. It slipped under Monica's glove and Kim advanced from second to third.

"Ugghh!" I muttered under my breath. I was so frustrated. On the next pitch, Coach Moody called for a drop ball again. Mercy had an easy time making contact with this one. She bounced the low pitch into the dirt, and raced to first with a single. Kim scored from third easily. Cougars 2, Monarchs 0.

When the ball returned to my glove I waved Monica toward the mound. I spoke to her in a sharp whisper. "I don't care what Mrs. Moody calls. We're throwing rise balls to the next batter—fastballs to the batter after that. You got it?" Frustration was all over my face, and my competitive juices were flowing. I was embarrassing myself and it was all Mrs. Moody's fault. If she couldn't make the right calls, I would. Monica nodded her helmet-heavy head in agreement.

My game plan worked to perfection. The next batter popped up my rise ball for the second out. The batter after that struck out on three straight fastballs. Calling my own pitches and getting two easy outs made me twice as mad. It was as if Coach Moody wanted to lose! When I got to the dugout, I walked right past Mrs. Moody. I threw my mitt under the bench. Then I grabbed a helmet and walked over to the on-deck circle. I was the leadoff batter this inning.

Before I reached the plate, Mrs. Moody hollered toward the end of the bench. "Traci, get a bat! You're pinch hitting for Selena." Then she looked directly at me, "Selena, have a seat."

I froze in my tracks. "But I—"

She cut me off. "There's only one coach on this team, Selena, and it's not you." Her voice was cold and her dark eyes stared straight at me. "Now have a seat."

Mrs. Moody didn't care that I had the second-best batting average on the team. She didn't care that the score was still close in this game. She only cared about proving her point. I found my way to the far end of the dugout. Traci had already dug her cleats into the batter's box. Sitting on the bench, I removed my Jose Valentine batting gloves. My day was over.

A few of my teammates slid next to me. They asked the same questions that spun around in my head: *Who would pitch the next inning? Does Coach Moody want to lose?* The truth was, she didn't care about the outcome of this game. She only cared that I got her message: "There's only one coach on this team, and it's not you." I held back my tears. Her message was ringing through loud and clear.

From the bench, I watched us lose that game 15-1.

When I came home that night, I grabbed Mom's pillow and ran into her room. I cried on the bed for awhile. Although four years had passed since her death, Mom's sweet fragrance remained on the pillow. Her absence never got easier for me—especially when I was upset.

In the middle of my sobs, a knock on the front door was a welcome sound. It was Victoria. She was stopping by to hear how the game had gone. She wasn't able to be there because of her night class. My red eyes gave her a clue that the ship hadn't sailed smoothly. We sat together in the kitchen and shared a bowl of cookie dough ice cream. In her usual way, Victoria listened to my complaints about Mrs. Moody. I told her that I was thinking about quitting the team. I just couldn't handle playing for Mrs. Moody any longer.

In between spoonfuls, Victoria offered her advice. "I understand your frustration." She put her arm over my shoulder. "Mrs. Moody definitely doesn't make all the right choices. Still, she *is* your coach. When you joined the team, you made the decision to play for her. Mrs. Moody, with all her faults, *is* the boss. You won't win a battle with her." She lifted both her palms up in a matter-of-fact manner. Mom used to do the same thing. For a moment I felt her in the room with us. A lump of ice cream slid down my throat. I was choked up and tried to squeeze back the tears. Victoria continued, "I went through some tough times with coaches, too. I hated my college coach. He'd yell at me and make stupid coaching mistakes. Believe me, I thought about quitting—but I didn't quit. Sticking with softball turned out to be a great decision for me. You're not a quitter either, Selena." Victoria smiled. "Besides, you know you can't *really* quit. You love it way too much."

As I sat there eating spoonful after spoonful of ice cream, I realized that Victoria was right. High school softball had been a bumpy ride so far. But there was no way I could ever quit playing the sport I loved. I would just have to deal with Mrs. Moody. Eventually, I'd get a coach that I liked. The question was—when?

CHAPTER EIGHT

TWO SURPRISES

With a week left in my freshman season, I celebrated my fifteenth birthday. Dad told me we were going to have a small party at a local reception hall. He said he would invite about ten people to join us. It sounded like fun and seemed like a great way to get my mind off of Mrs. Moody. There were just three games left in my freshman season. And I know it sounds bad, but I was relieved it was ending.

Victoria agreed to drive me down to the hall. Dad said he wouldn't be able to meet us until after work. As we pulled into the parking lot, I wondered if he'd invited girls from my team. "That would be cool," I told Victoria, "it would be a chance for us to sit down and talk—just a bunch of girls eating pizza and hanging out." Victoria smiled at my comments.

We casually walked toward the front entrance

and I walked in without a second thought.

"Surprise!"

Bright lights flashed as I stepped through the door. After my eyes adjusted to the lights, I smiled and turned a deep cherry red. The room seemed to spin in circles. Everyone I had ever known stood in front of me. I had never been so surprised or excited in my life. There were loud cheers, whistling and clapping all directed at me! Standing in shock, I looked toward an area of the room which had a stage. Hanging in between loads of gold and white balloons, was a sign. It read: "Happy Birthday Selena!"

Dad was the first person to meet me at the door as I walked through it. Dressed in a navy blue suit and tie, he wrapped his arms around me. When he drew away, his eyes welled up with tears. He gently held my face in his hands. "This is your day, baby girl!"

It was my fifteenth birthday, which meant that it was time for my quinceañera. The quinceañera is a celebration of a girl's entrance into womanhood. Hispanic girls all over the world celebrate this occasion. Dad and I had talked about this day last month. He had me convinced that we were skipping the traditions and just having pizza. Boy, did he fool me. This was a real quinceañera party. Dad had gone all out—from elaborate decorations, to the band that was setting up in the corner.

After Mom's death, Dad had changed his priorities. He had worked with his boss and shifted his work hours as much as possible. This enabled him to spend more time with us. He acted as a mother and a father for me and my brothers. He attended our games, did laundry, and worked 50 hours a week to support us. I wanted him to know how much all that meant to me.

As Dad and I released our embrace, he handed me a beautiful pink gown. Pink is the traditional color a girl wears on her quinceañera. Victoria looked over at me and smiled. I knew right away that she'd helped Dad pick the dress out. My eyes lit up as I ran my fingers down the lace fabric. "Wow! It's beautiful!" I kissed Dad on the cheek and shot a smile toward Victoria.

The next stop was the girl's restroom. I quickly changed out of my jeans. Then I put on the dress and a pair of ballerina slippers. Victoria added a few curls to my hair and brightened my face with blush, mascara and lipstick. When I looked in the mirror even I was surprised by my transformation. I exited the bathroom and entered the hall, bowing my head in embarrassment. The fifty-plus people hooted, howled and cheered at my appearance. I managed to keep my chin up and not look too nervous. I should have been used to being the center of attention by now. After all, I was a pitcher. People were always staring at me on the softball field.

When we finished the traditional quinceañera service, I greeted each of the guests. Their faces represented so many parts of my life. Coach Frank Fisher from my first baseball team stood with his wife. I gave Coach Larry Shepard, from the Orange Crush, a hug next. Tons of my former teammates were there, including Anne Fishburn, Elizabeth Lee and Monica Larson. Family flooded around me, too. Joe and Carlos and some of my cousins from Mexico were all in attendance.

A live band started the festivities off with a special song. The first dance of the quinceañera is shared by the birthday girl and her father. So Dad and I stepped onto the dance floor together. He held me tight and waltzed me around the room. "You look beautiful," he whispered. All the guests encircled us, snapping pictures and swaying to the beat.

The next dance was with my brothers. In typical fashion, they fought over me. Eventually, my older brother, Joe, won out. After Joe dipped and spun me dizzy, he and Carlos traded spots. I laughed and screamed through the entire song.

Following the dances, I sat down in a chair in the middle of a circle of people. Then I stretched my feet out from under my floor-length dress. Dad would be removing my slippers and replacing them with high heels. This ritual symbolized the change from childhood to womanhood. I dropped my head back and belted out an embarrassed laugh. High heels were not in my wardrobe!

Before Dad could slip on the pink, satin heels,

Victoria entered the circle. She interrupted us. "Excuse me Mr. Garcia, can I make a slight change?" Dad obviously knew about this prank, as he eagerly stepped out of the way. Victoria knelt down, set a shoebox on the ground, and lifted off the top. With a grin she showed the crowd a pair of brand-new, black leather cleats. The room erupted in laughter as Victoria slipped them onto my feet.

Playing along with the joke, I pranced around in a circle like a model. As I walked, I felt a sense of freedom inside of me. I really *was* turning into a woman. Quietly, I had always feared that I would never feel like a woman. After Mom passed away, I was sure that I'd never learn how to be beautiful or ladylike. What did Dad or Joe or Carlos know about that stuff? But Victoria came into my life, and through her I found a balance.

The amazing evening continued. There was dancing, delicious food, and great conversations. The band sung a Spanish rendition of Happy Birthday— *Feliz Compleaño*—before I blew out all fifteen candles. The final event of the night was the best part. While I stood chatting with Anne and Elizabeth, Dad walked over. He reached inside his suit coat and pulled out a small, wrapped box. He handed it to me and smiled. The music stopped. "This is for you, Selena."

I cradled the box in my hand like an egg. I tilted my head to my shoulder. "Dad, what are you doing?"

"Just open it, Selena." Dad smiled.

I pulled off the white satin ribbon and slowly peeled back the wrapping paper. Then I opened the velvet box carefully. Mom's wedding ring was inside, shining like a star. It was beautiful. I looked up at Dad, unable to speak. I could only wrap my arms around him and cry. Dad, too, was weeping as he whispered into my ear, "Your mother was amazing." He paused, barely able to speak without crying. "She would want you to wear this." Despite Mom's absence, the love surrounding me that night filled me with happiness.

Two weeks after my party, I finished my freshman softball season. There were times that year when I thought I'd never play softball again. I barely made it through with Mrs. Moody as my coach. Yet because I loved the game, I was ready and willing to play another season under her "expert" guidance. I wouldn't let her stop me from reaching my dream.

Luckily, miracles do happen. One week into the summer before my sophomore year, I got some great news. Mrs. Moody had quit as the softball coach. That wasn't even the best of it—Victoria had been offered the job! She was hired as an English teacher *and* a softball coach at Monte Vista High. The first day of school couldn't come soon enough.

Even though softball season was nearly six months away, I spent every afternoon on the diamond. Monica Larson, Roselee Rivera, and myself, agreed to help Victoria fix up the field. We raked new dirt in the infield and planted seeds in the outfield. The field definitely needed a facelift. We felt like artists as we touched up the benches, pulled weeds and repaired the outfield fence.

The biggest transformation came in the batting cage. Last season, we had named it "The Dungeon." It was dark and dusty and smelled weird. Plus, pieces of net hung down all over the small, chain-link enclosed area. Often times our bats would get stuck in the netting. Dozens of balls got caught in the loose webbing, too. So we helped Victoria tie back the loose nets. We oiled up the rickety pitching machine as well. When we were finished, the place actually looked pretty good.

Our reward for helping Victoria was huge. She gave us a key to the batting cage and we were allowed to hit for as long and as often as we wanted. I hit more balls that off-season than I had in all my years of playing softball. It really showed once the regular season began.

The first game of my sophomore season was nothing like my freshman year. We were a really good team and we played with confidence. Our dominating 10-0 victory was a great way to kick things off. I pitched a shutout, striking out six helpless batters. Plus, I finished 3-for-4 with two doubles. I couldn't have asked for a better start.

That entire sophomore season was like a dream. With Victoria running the show, our team posted the best record in school history, 15-6. Although we lost early in the playoffs, our season was a major success. People at school began recognizing the softball team. We became known as one of the top programs. Everyone started asking me about my future plans with the sport. I hadn't given it much thought, aside from knowing that I wanted a scholarship. College seemed very far away to me.

But a look through the mailbox one day made me realize that college was right around the corner. Hidden in the middle of some junk mail was a letter from the University of Horizon. I opened it and read the words: "...interested in you as a college softball student-athlete." My heart beat wildly. The letters continued to trickle in, following a successful season of club softball.

By the time my junior season began, college coaches were at most of our games. They usually sat in the stands right behind the dugout. They were easily within my view as I pitched. I tried not to notice them, but it was hard. I couldn't believe that coaches were showing up at Monte Vista high to watch *me* play!

Having been through this process herself, Victoria knew how to handle it. She never told me before our games if coaches were coming. There was no reason to add to the pressure I felt. She did inform me afterward, though. Although her guidance was great, the most effective tool I had against the pressure was in my back pocket. Victoria understood the power of Mom's prayer card too. She helped me use that inspiration when I needed it most. If I seemed frazzled on the field, Victoria would pat her back pocket. This always reminded me that I was playing a *game*. No matter where softball took me, Mom would be proud. That thought eased any tension I was feeling.

Six years after her death, I still longed to touch my mother. But life went on without Maria Nora Garcia. It had to. I still refused to pull my hair up in a ponytail or tie it with bows and ribbons. Dad was right, though, I was becoming more like Mom each day. I even started cooking some of her specialties in the kitchen. Seeing the looks on my brother's faces when I pulled tamales from the oven made it all worthwhile. Like Mom, I began to appreciate the simple things: dinners with Dad, long talks with Victoria, and even an occasional movie night with Joe and Carlos.

On the softball field, Victoria's coaching style brought out the best in me. That much was clear in the final game of the season, my best performance of the year. Although we missed the playoffs, we finished on a high note. I allowed just one run in the season finale. I struck out a season-high twelve batters. We won the game 8-1 and I knocked in three of the runs myself. I completed the season with a 12-3 record and batted .454. I earned another varsity letter and was named a member of the first team All-County squad.

Following the final game, three college coaches

were waiting to talk with me. Victoria spoke to the coaches before introducing me to each of them separately. They congratulated me on a great season and all expressed interest in my future plans. I responded just as Victoria had told me to. I gave a solid, confident handshake, listened and looked them directly in the eyes.

To pretend I wasn't excited would be like a bear saying he didn't like honey. The thought of playing *college* softball blew me away. No one in my family had ever attended a four-year college, let alone for free! Going to college on a softball scholarship seemed amazing, unbelievable—fantastic!

This dream drove me daily. I couldn't go twenty-four hours without swinging a bat or throwing a ball. At home, much of my free time consisted of going through a shoebox filled with recruiting letters. I lined up a top-ten list of schools each night. That list seemed to change with the wind. I soon found out that the winds of change can bite you.

CHAPTER NINE

CINDERELLA SUPERESTRELLA

On the last day of my junior year, I dressed for my final gym class. LuAnn Gores, our starting catcher next season, was in that class, too. LuAnn was a great athlete, especially when it came to basketball. She was a speedy point guard who had a silky smooth jump shot. I knew she was better than me on the hardwood, but I still felt that I was as fast as she was. So when she challenged me to a race, I gladly accepted.

A handful of girls who knew us stuck around. Even our teacher, Mr. Silva, watched from the side-line. When he blew his whistle LuAnn and I both blasted off the baseline. We agreed to run one "suicide." A suicide means running to the free-throw line and back, to the half-court line and back, the far free-throw line and back, and then to the full court line and back.

I reached the first free-throw line before LuAnn.

Then I raced back to the baseline. When I planted my right foot to turn around, though, my shoe stuck to the floor. My momentum carried me forward and a snapping sound echoed throughout the gym. I felt my ankle roll sideways. Instantly, I fell to the floor.

The gym fell silent. My whimpering provided the only trace of noise. Mr. Silva quickly ran to my aid as LuAnn sprinted toward me. "Are you alright, Selena?" He knelt down beside me. I planted my face into the floor and wriggled around in pain.

"It really, really hurts." I moaned as tears streamed down my cheeks.

LuAnn responded, "I'll get Victoria."

Mr. Silva convinced me to sit upright as he sent a student to fetch a bag of ice. The pain in my ankle was as bad as any pain I could remember. My gut feeling told me that this injury was bad. Within two minutes, Victoria came running through the gym doors. She bent down and put her hand on my back. "What happened, Selena?"

I dropped my head in my lap, trying to clear my throat. "I think I just lost my scholarship."

My stupid race with LuAnn left me with a torn tendon in my right ankle. It also left me with a giant, smelly, and *not* softball-friendly cast. My senior season was around the corner, and I wasn't sure if I'd be ready.

As news of my injury spread, many colleges

that had been hot on my trail dropped interest. The mailman placed fewer and fewer letters in our box. Only Jason Lebot from the College of the Pines was still writing to me. He would send notes about once a month. Coach Jason kept up with my progress, but never went as far as offering me a scholarship. He represented my only hope. This hope, combined with Victoria's support, kept me going.

Every day during that summer, Victoria picked me up and brought me to work with her at Monte Vista High. I knew I was fighting against the odds, but I wouldn't quit. So while Victoria taught summer school, I worked out. I fought against my annoying ankle cast in the small gym. Sometimes I lifted weights for my upper body. Other times I tried to ride the stationary bike. On some afternoons Victoria took me down on the field and I hit buckets of balls off a tee. Doing anything softball related made me feel great.

Late at night, my ankle would hurt badly. The cast wrapped around my leg seemed like the heaviest weight on earth. Being injured was hard on me. If I only could have avoided that stupid race, I would have had my scholarship. Thoughts like these kept me awake at night. They also made me train twice as hard.

Keeping my pitching arm sharp was the hardest part of my training. I could throw overhand without much of a problem, but the windmill motion was tough. That's because softball pitching requires tons of lower body strength. It wasn't until the final two weeks of summer that I could actually step on the mound. With my cast still on, I was forced to stand upright. The ball came off my hand wildly, and I found little control. I threw about twenty pitches a day just to keep my arm loose. Without my legs at full strength, though, my workouts were limited. I never doubted myself more than I did on those days.

Finally the day came to get that stupid, uncomfortable thing off my leg. As I sat on the doctor's table I felt like a prisoner about to be released. The cast came off and I nearly cried. Beneath the cotton gauze wrap was my stiff right ankle and a tiny, shrunken calf muscle. The smell of my leg nearly made me throw up. A shower became my first priority.

My next job was rehab. With my confidence at its lowest point, I got to work. It was hard for me to believe I would ever be the same pitcher I was before my injury. I performed exercises and stretches four times a day. Plus, Victoria, myself, and a few of my teammates ran sprints in the outfield in the afternoons. This helped me get my wind back. Taking some swings in the batting cages had me thinking positively by mid-winter. After awhile I was crushing the ball again!

Although it was a slow process, my right ankle rebounded. By the beginning of my senior season, I felt close to one hundred percent. It had been nine months since my injury had occurred. I rehabbed so hard that I honestly felt stronger than ever. Mentally, though, I still wasn't sure whether I could come back and be a dominant pitcher. Doubts filled my brain like weeds in a garden.

Victoria had just the right solution. I had no class during seventh period, so I visited the softball field every day. When I got there, I would repaint the bases with bright white paint. Then I would paint the pitcher's mound. Moving the brush back and forth was like therapy. My mind focused on the strokes of my brush rather than the pressures of success or failure. Painting was simple and relaxing. It worked so well that I put a paintbrush in my duffel bag for road games. Everyone thought I was crazy. On the team bus, I would swish the brush back and forth through the air for the entire ride.

Any doubts I had about my ability vanished when we opened our season 6-0. I was the winning pitcher in three of the games. Twice, I had shut our opponents out completely. My pitching arm was stronger than ever due to my rehab weightlifting. Plus, after spending time in a cast, I had learned an important lesson: my legs were the key to pitching. Victoria had been telling me this since our first lesson, but it had never really sunk in. Not until I was forced to practice pitching without them, that is.

I began to use my legs much more efficiently that season. Strangely, I was throwing the ball harder than I had in the past. This was an unexpected benefit of my injury. Suddenly, I was the hardest-throwing pitcher in our section.

We finished that season with an amazing 15-3 record. We were first in our league and a sure bet to make the playoffs. Despite our team's great success, college coaches rarely came to see our games. My injury, combined with the small town I lived in, were both reasons they stayed away. It really made me sad at times. I knew I was good enough to pitch in college. If I got the chance, I could really help a college team. I also knew that paying tuition was going to be hard on Dad. He had promised me he would find a way to send me. But I desperately wanted to give him the gift of a scholarship.

With Victoria's encouragement, I remained upbeat about the empty seats in the stands. Her advice was to simply enjoy my final season. And I did. Sometimes, though, the situation weighed on me. A thousand times, I wished I'd never run that race against LuAnn. If I hadn't, my life would be different.

Once the playoffs began, I put those negative thoughts out of my mind. This was my last chance to show anybody who was watching how good I was. We got off to a great start. Our bats and gloves shined in a first-round 10-2 win. In the quarterfinals, I took care of business on the mound. I threw a four-hitter in a 6-1 victory. We faced our toughest test in the semis, but won 3-2 over our rivals, the Del Ray Cougars. That set up a showdown against tradition-rich Ponderosa High. The winner would take home the County Championship Cup—a trophy Monte Vista High had never won.

The last game of my high school career finally arrived on a hot day in early June. I had given up worrying at that point. All that was left to do was go out a winner. Victoria asked the maintenance crew at the field if I could arrive before the game and paint the bases. They had no problem with that. I drove Victoria's car to the field three hours before the game. When I reached the field I started painting first base—then second and third base in order. With each stroke of the brush I visualized myself connecting for a single, a double and a triple. I was rounding each of the bases, pumping my arms, sliding, diving, jumping and winning.

Next, I took the paint can and brush to the mound. As I glossed over the worn rubber, I pictured myself exploding off the mound with my left foot, and dragging my right foot. I imagined each of my pitches: hot fastballs, sick curves, dramatic drops, quick rises and confusing changeups. I pictured them all coming off my hand smoothly as I finished with an uplifting follow through. My last project was to polish home plate. There, I visualized batters frozen in their stance as fastballs whizzed by them. I pictured hitters swinging helplessly through a deadly drop.

Minutes before the game started, I relieved my nerves by taking long and deep breaths. I was swishing my cleats across the many drops of paint I'd spilled in the dirt. Then, I shocked all of my teammates. I dug inside my bag and pulled out gold and maroon hair ribbons. Ribbons and bows were part of my history— a history that ended when Mom passed away. I stared at the ribbons for a few seconds, taking a moment to breathe.

I hollered down the bench to my fashion-friendly teammate, Liz Williams. She always wore lots of makeup and looked pretty on game days. "Hey Lizzy, can you give me one of your high-style braid jobs?"

When I spoke these words, all of my teammates froze in their tracks and stared at me. They knew the reason for my free-flowing hair. Ever since Mom died, I refused to wear bows, ribbons or even ponytails. My hair got in the way and blew out of control at times, but my teammates had always understood. The deep memory tied to my mom and my long locks was something I cherished.

"I want the works, Lizzy." I spoke clearly as Liz walked toward me.

As she braided my hair, Victoria came by. "I guess Superestrella Cinderella is in order today, huh?" Victoria had learned of my Bobby Sox nickname at my quinceañera. Until today, she had never used it.

After Liz had tied the last knot, I huddled all the players around me. We stood in front of the dugout and I made a final comment. "This is the biggest game of our lives. We own this field, guys. Let's play like it."

I ran out to the mound with a spring in my step.

I felt lighter and freer as my hair was less scratchy on the neck. I hadn't worn my hair like this since the first time I ever pitched. That was nearly six years ago. When I reached the rubber, I heard a familiar sound. Someone was shaking a can filled with rocks in the crowd. My heart raced and I glanced toward the stands as if Mom would be sitting there. Instead, I smiled at my dad, sitting with my brothers. He was shaking Mom's rock-filled soda can and screaming, "Go Selena, go! Go Selena, go!"

Slightly embarrassed, I bowed my head in appreciation of my family. I glanced over to the crowd one last time. I spotted Jason Lebot, the coach from the College of the Pines. We made eye contact and then I looked away. I didn't recognize any other college coaches in the stands. Seeing him there made my heart jump, but I quickly calmed down. I was determined to let nothing—not even college—interfere with this special moment in my life. My final high school softball game would be my greatest game. I would give all of my strength and all of my positive energy to win this one. I was going to leave everything I had out on that field.

Ready, locked and loaded, I stared into LuAnn's glove. The first Ponderosa batter stepped to the plate. I tucked my right elbow in, pulled my shoulders back and made a deep bend at the knees. Then, with all my might, I windmilled the game's first pitch. The fastest ball I'd ever thrown buzzed right down the middle.

The hitter stood staring—like a statue. I followed that pitch with a sharp rise and then a baffling changeup. I needed just three pitches to record my first strikeout. I fanned eight more batters in the next five innings. I had found an unbelievable groove. I felt like a fighter pilot using radar to land pinpoint-placement missiles.

Unfortunately, our bats were silent. Heading into the top of the seventh, we faced a scoreless tie. Ponderosa brought up the top of its order. For the first time that day, I walked the leadoff batter. I'd allowed just two hits the entire game so far. Fortunately, the next two batters grounded out. This left a runner on first with two outs.

Ponderosa depended on its cleanup hitter to come through. She'd collected both of their hits—each on outside drop pitches. LuAnn signaled for an inside fastball. I nodded my head in agreement. The Ponderosa slugger grunted as she swung. She ripped a sharp grounder right at our shortstop, Jenni Del Cruz. Unfortunately, the hard shot went through Jenni's legs and rolled into the outfield.

The runner at first base had left the bag before I tossed the pitch to the plate. By the time the ball got through Jenni's legs, she was rounding second. Amazingly, as the ball reached our center fielder, Suzie Dime, the speedy runner was on her way home. A laser beam came from short center field and beat the runner by ten feet. LuAnn applied the tag easily. With a sigh of relief we sprinted off the field. We were hoping to win the title in our last at-bat. To our surprise, though, the umpires had gathered in a circle around second base. Within minutes they called our team back on the field. They ruled that our shortstop had interfered with the Ponderosa runner. We were all stunned.

I stared at the scoreboard from the pitcher's mound. Ponderosa had been awarded a run. They took a 1-0 lead. Before I knew what had happened, Victoria was out on the field. She displayed an anger I'd never seen from her before. I couldn't hear what she was saying, but her bright red face showed how mad she was. Victoria left the field shaking her head. She gathered us all together along the first-base line. "Don't let the umpires take this game from you! Let's get one more out and finish this thing off with our bats."

I took a minute to cool down behind the mound. I fixed my visor and took a deep breath. After tightening one of my hair ribbons, I looked into LuAnn's glove and focused again.

First pitch, fastball, strike one.

Second pitch, curveball, strike two.

Third pitch, drop ball outside, strike three, side retired—again.

The bad call from the umpires really got our dugout going. We were yelling and screaming as the top of the order came to the plate. We still had a chance at the championship. Now it was payback time! Our leadoff batter, Marla Montez, approached the plate. Just three pitches into the at-bat, she slap-bunted a single down the line. The throw to first base wasn't even close. She clapped her hands and the cheering in our dugout got louder.

Our number two hitter popped out and quieted every one down for a moment. Then I stepped to the plate and stared down the pitcher. This was my opportunity to get revenge. Before digging my cleats into the batter's box, I knelt down to tighten my shoelaces. I adjusted my Jose Valentine batting gloves—the same gloves I'd worn since my meeting with the slugger.

During my last at bat, I had ripped an inside pitch. So this time I waited for an outside fastball. Prepared, I choked up on the bat and decided to go with the pitch. Sure enough, the heater headed for the outside half of the plate. Using a short, quick swing I lined a shot the opposite way into the right-center gap. Our leadoff hitter, Marla Montez, raced all the way home from first. I sailed into second base, clapping my hands in celebration. The game was tied 1-1.

With one out, Jill Hart stepped up to the plate. She was hoping to deliver the knockout punch. At 6-feet, 160-pounds, she was a force at the plate. She definitely intimidated opposing pitchers. Jill had a reputation for her power. In this at-bat, though, she suffered a power outage—striking out on three pitches.

So with one chance left, our championship hopes fell on the shoulders of LuAnn. This was the same LuAnn who I'd raced, and lost to, in a big way.

LuAnn and I had become close friends since my accident. I was excited she was at the plate. I believed in her. She was a gifted athlete who carried herself with confidence. In high-pressure situations, she was cool and confident.

With two outs, I would be running on contact. My heart raced excitedly. LuAnn got ahead in the count 2-0. So the next pitch was very important. The Ponderosa pitcher delivered a fastball right down the middle. LuAnn teed off on it as if she knew what was coming. She lined the pitch back up the middle, just out of the reach of Ponderosa's second baseman.

I broke on the ping of the bat, heading for third. My eyes focused on Victoria. She stood a fourth of the way down the line, screaming: "Go! Go! Go!" She was waving me home!

As I sprinted toward the plate I noticed Ponderosa's catcher attempting to block my path. For a moment, I imagined a collision with the fully geared catcher. I thought about re-injuring my ankle. Within a blink of an eye, though, that fear disappeared. I dropped down into an aggressive slide, leading with my right leg. I reached the plate just as the catcher pulled down the throw. She reached down and tried to tag my chest. I managed to touch the outside of the plate with my hand. I looked up at the umpire with hope in my eyes. "Safe! Safe! Safe!" he yelled as he waved his arms across his body.

Before I could rise from the dust, my teammates jumped on me. We formed a huge pile of teen-age girls on home plate. Although the weight pressing down on me felt heavy, I couldn't have been more excited. I was safe at home, and we were number one!

CHAPTER TEN

SAFE AT HOME

LuAnn and I walked to the locker-room a short time after our dog pile at the plate. We laughed about how nervous we both were in our final at-bats. Then we talked about the excitement of having just one day left of high school. LuAnn was going to play basketball at Mammoth College in Tucson. Silently I sulked, knowing that I had just twenty-four hours to sign a college scholarship. This was about as likely as getting struck by lightning at this point.

We passed by Victoria's office window on the way to our lockers. Victoria was sitting at her desk across from a man wearing a forest green baseball cap. My eyes met with Victoria's through the glass. She stood up smiling, and waved me into her office.

I patted LuAnn on the back and I walked into the small room. Victoria guided me through the door.

"Someone's here to see you." She spoke excitedly and right away I felt that something was up.

The man with the green hat stood up and turned around to face me. To my delight, it was Coach Jason Lebot from the College of the Pines. He greeted me with a hearty handshake.

He smiled at me. "You played a great game out there, Selena."

I shook my head humbly. "Thank you very much." Although my mouth spoke these words, my brain was out of order. I simply could not focus on this conversation—not until I knew what he was doing in Victoria's office. This thought buzzed through me like an electric shock. Coach Jason adjusted his cap, "So what are your plans for celebrating the big win?"

Celebrating the big win? I thought. *What does that matter? Does he mean celebrate because it is my last win?* My heart continued racing. *Why was he in Victoria's office? Why had she called me in here?* "I'm not sure." I answered, "My dad's supposed to meet me here in a few minutes. Maybe he'll have something planned." I was barely paying attention to the words that flowed from my mouth.

Coach Jason took a step closer to me. "Well, he's going to be real happy when you tell him the great news."

"What news?" I asked.

"The news about your softball scholarship to

the College of the Pines."

"Oh." I stopped myself, unsure of what I had just heard. "Wait, what did you just say?" I smiled from ear to ear, realizing exactly what he had said.

Coach Lebot repeated himself anyway. "Your softball scholarship to the College of the Pines." He spoke the words again. "If you're interested, that is."

Instead of answering I half-screamed, half-laughed and half-cried. It was a really strange noise. Then I yelped, "Of course!"

Dad arrived right on cue at Victoria's door. He took his hat off as he entered, shaking hands with Coach Lebot. "What's all the shouting about?" Dad asked with a look of confused excitement on his face.

Victoria gave him a handshake-turned-hug. "Hi Mr. Garcia." She then pointed in my direction. "Selena has something to tell you."

I turned and looked Dad in the eyes, "Dad, I'm going to college. I'm going to play softball on a scholarship. It's all free!"

Dad was silent at first. Then he grabbed a chair and sat down. I never saw him look so happy or so proud. "You did it," he whispered. "I can't believe what you did." He stared directly into my eyes when he said, "You don't quit, Selena. You're just like your mother." He kissed me on the forehead and sat back down, laughing.

I would cherish those words, and that moment, forever.

The car ride home that afternoon was so much fun. Dad was driving and Joe was sitting in the front seat with Carlos and I in the back. We left the parking lot and Dad kept shouting out the window, "My baby's going to college!" As usual, I was embarrassed. Joe and Carlos were shaking Mom's rock-filled soda can and music was blasting. I don't think I had ever smiled so big.

When we got back to our apartment Joe and Carlos were still full of energy. They asked me if I wanted to head down to The Field for a catch. I was surprised by the offer, especially because it came from Joe. We hadn't all played catch together in a long time. I probably hadn't been on The Field in close to three years.

We grabbed our mitts and a baseball. The sun was about to set, so we had to hurry. When we got down to the field I had to laugh. Joe was bossing Carlos and me around the same way he did when we were kids. "Carlos, you stand by first base. Selena, you line up by home plate." He looked up at the sun. "Hurry up." Some things never changed.

We played catch together for about thirty minutes as the sun faded. It was the perfect end to the perfect day: I was going to college. Dad didn't have to pay a giant tuition bill. We had won the championship game, and I was back on the Field, playing catch with my brothers. The only thing missing was Mom.

Carlos threw a laser and the pop of my mitt

echoed across the diamond. The echo was familiar, but it was a noise I hadn't heard in a while. I couldn't remember the last time I had thrown a baseball. The popping sound of a softball hitting the center of a mitt is totally different. When a softball lands in your glove, the pop is hollow. It seems to last longer than the quick pop of a baseball, too. Before the large ball hits, there is a low *whoosh* as it makes contact with the leather. These two sounds represented two different stages in my life. I tossed the baseball over to Joe as hard as I could.

He laughed, "Jeez, Selena, you've got one heck of an arm."

At that moment, listening to Joe compliment me, I truly realized how much life had changed. I also realized how weird a baseball felt in my hand. It was tiny and hard and heavy. When I threw it, the feeling was strange. I remembered the first time I'd ever thrown a softball. I hated it. The ball felt big and soft and light. I wondered how I would ever be able to throw it with any accuracy. I never imagined myself getting used to that giant ball. Now, holding a tiny baseball in my hands, I realized that I was truly a softball player. My transformation was complete.

My eyes glanced all over the Field as we continued to toss the baseball back and forth. The Field was exactly the same as when I was a kid. I laughed when I looked at the parked cars a few feet from right field. The splintery wood fence and the giant holes lining the outfield were still there too. "How did we ever play on this field?" I asked my brothers.

Carlos had the perfect answer, "Why did we ever stop?"

Three and a half months after that final high school game, it was time to go. With Dad's old pickup stuffed with bags, bats and boxes, we began the long trip to Utah. That would be the site of my home for the next four years. Dad had volunteered to drive me. Joe and Carlos offered to come, but there was no room for them in the packed truck.

Instead, we said goodbye in the family room. Joe told me to stay away from the boys, Carlos demanded I keep my eye on the ball. Then Joe got serious for a second, which hardly ever happened. "If you have any problems, you just let me know. I'll be up there that day if you need me." He smiled, "I'll miss you, girl." Then he got up from the couch and lifted me off the ground in his arms.

Carlos got up from the couch next. In his sensitive way, he kissed me on the cheek. Then he spoke softly, "I'm gonna miss you, too. Who's gonna sit between me and Jose at dinner now?" I tried not to cry when Carlos made this comment. "Don't forget to call us." He kissed my cheek again as Dad and I walked out the door.

With tears in my eyes, I began the greatest adventure of my life.

Dad and I dropped by Victoria's house next. Although I felt overjoyed by my journey, I couldn't hide my deep sadness. I just hated leaving Victoria behind. While Dad waited in the car, I sat next to Victoria and thanked her over and over again. Her guidance, her trust, her advice, her encouragement and her friendship had changed my life. She spoke with tears in her eyes. "I love you, sister. I'll be at your first weekend fall tournament. I promise." A minute later, she was waving as we pulled out of her driveway.

We still had one more stop to make on my goodbye tour. Dad drove us to the top of Eternal Mountain, the burial site of my mother. As we walked in between the tombstones, I became emotional right away. We reached Mom's plot and I knelt down beside it. Then I lost it, crying hard for a moment. With Dad standing a few feet behind me, I rubbed my hand across her name—Maria Nora Garcia. I put a flower on the top of her stone and sat on the soft grass. Dad sat next to me.

"I know you're with me, Mom." I reached inside my backpack and pulled out a couple of items: he hair ribbon I wore in the County Championship game, a copy of the newspaper article from that game, and the large ball point pen I had used to sign my scholarship. I laid everything out beside her stone. "I know you're proud of me, too." I wiped away my tears. "I can't wait to see what happens next. I still love you." You see, that's the thing about death—it can't take away your love. It took me a long time to realize that. After Dad said a few words to Mom, we made our way back to the car.

The journey to Rising Road, Utah, went quickly. Dad went over my schedule and gave me fatherly advice. I'd never heard him talk so much! It was like *he* was going to college! Before I knew it, we were only an hour away.

As we crossed the border into Utah, Dad had one more thing to say. "Selena, you're the first person in our family to go to college—and on a scholarship!" He slapped my leg in excitement, then paused. "I know I haven't been able to buy you a lot of things. I know I haven't taken you a lot of places, either. I wish I could have done more for you guys." He paused, "Your mother, if she were here—"

I cut Dad off, "She would be so proud of you, Dad. You kept our family together." There was more I wanted to say. But as we turned onto Pines Road the only words I could speak were, "Wow, there it is!"

We both stared at the beautiful buildings that stood before us. The college was more impressive than I had imagined. I pointed out my window at the giant clock tower in the center of campus. I'd never seen the school in person before. I'd only flipped through pictures in catalogs. After weaving though brick buildings and fraternity houses, we found the athletic department. Coach Lebot's office was just inside the front door.

A moment later, we stood face-to-face with Coach Lebot. "Hi, Selena!" He extended his hand. "Glad you made it here safely."

During the next thirty minutes Coach took us on a tour of the facilities. College of the Pines competed at the Division 1 level—the highest level college sports had to offer. We passed by the campus trophy case, loaded with conference title plaques. We then entered the state-of-the-art weight room. Next, Coach used his keys to open the softball locker room.

Forest-green lockers bordered the beautifully carpeted room. Hanging in each locker was a bright white jersey. I walked to the nearest stall and turned the uniform around. GARCIA 31 was stitched there. Of course I started crying again. I couldn't hold in my excitement. I was living in a dream, but it was real. "This is so cool!" I said. I remembered the day I'd walked through the Scorpions locker-room. That day I dreamed of finding my name on a locker stall—and stitched on the back of a jersey. That dream had become a reality.

We exited the building and headed outside for our final destination—Forest Field. The chilly night weather of the fall season sent goose bumps down my body. I had become used to the heat of Arizona. I realized then that my move to Utah meant completely different weather. I'd even get the chance to see snow in a few months! I slipped my hands into my pockets. I wondered how far we'd walk before I spotted the diamond. Two minutes later Coach Jason stopped us. "Go ahead and walk right up those stairs. The field is at the top. I'm gonna turn on the lights."

My heart was racing as we reached the top step. Then—like a bolt of lightning—the bright lights flashed on all around me. I blinked a few times. *Whoa,* I thought. Lush green grass in the outfield *and* the infield! A padded wall! Real red brick clay! Cement dugouts with heated seats! A bullpen covered for shade! *Two* batting cages with lights! A press box and an electronic scoreboard with video replay! "Whoa," I said aloud as I looked over at Dad.

I started to think about the Field in Tierra de Sueño again. I remembered sitting on top of that big rock, trying to get myself into a baseball game. Now look at me—this was really the big time.

"So what do you think, Selena?" Coach Jason's voice jolted me back to where I was.

"It's amazing." I spoke without looking away from the field.

Dad laughed and shook Coach Jason's hand.

Coach continued, "You guys are welcome to stay down here as long as you'd like. I've got to run, but I'll see you back here tomorrow for the first team meeting."

"You got it Coach." I nodded my head and grinned. "Thanks for showing us around."

Dad was hungry from the long ride. He left with Coach to pick up some dinner for us. I wanted to stay at the field a while longer. Dad agreed to come back and get me in an hour. As I sat in the dugout, I spotted a softball under the bench. I picked it up. As I rubbed it in my hands, I decided to make my way out to the mound.

Before reaching the rubber, I took off my jacket and tied it to the backstop fence behind home plate. It hung in what would be the heart of the strike zone. Arriving at the mound, I placed my feet on the rubber and set the ball in my right hand. As I eyed my red jacket, I paused, taking in the silence.

The quiet moment led me to ponder the past eighteen years of my life. I thought about Mom and the loss I had experienced. Her death had left a huge hole which could never be filled. I reached my hand into the back pocket of my pants and pulled out Mom's picture. I kissed it softly, knowing that she was with me at that very moment and everything was going to be alright.

Looking in toward the plate, I crouched down and pretended to see the catcher's sign. Like I'd done a thousand times before, I began to rock backwards. My eyes narrowed and my arm windmilled around. Then I pushed forward with my legs using all my might. With an upward follow-through, I flung the worn ball at the backstop. It smacked the heart of the jacket.

Instantly, I felt right at home.

TEST YOURSELF...ARE YOU A PROFESSIONAL READER?

Chapter 1: The Field

Describe The Field.

Why weren't errors tolerated in right field at The Field?

Besides an automatic invitation to The Field, what was the greatest reward Selena earned when she defeated Joe in the home run derby?

ESSAY

Until Selena thought up a plan, she wasn't even allowed to compete in the home run derby. How did this make her feel? Write about a time in your life when you were excluded. How did you feel?

Chapter 2: A Hard Call

Why didn't Selena want to play softball with the girls?

Name one aspect of playing baseball with the boys that Selena didn't enjoy.

What was the team's reaction to Selena's amazing double play? How did this reaction make her feel?

ESSAY

In this chapter, it becomes obvious that Selena is underappreciated by her teammates. Describe a situation in your life when you felt you didn't receive the recognition you deserved.

Chapter 3: A Changeup

What are a few reasons Selena enjoyed the switch from baseball to softball?

Why was Selena's mom so thrilled that Selena was enjoying her time on the softball team?

What was Selena's nickname? How did she acquire such a nickname?

ESSAY

In Chapter 3, Selena shows that your attitude can affect your performance. Describe a situation in your life when you mentally convinced yourself you could do something, and then did it. Why are positive thoughts so important?

Chapter 4: A Goodnight Kiss

What did Selena's mother mean by the expression "when you get lemons, you make lemonade"?

Why did Selena sometimes feel unlucky that she was a girl?

What seemed important to Selena after her mother passed away?

ESSAY

What do you think Selena's mother means by saying "that things never work out the way you plan them"? Give an example from your life of something not working out the way that you planned, yet eventually working out anyhow.

Chapter 5: A Challenge

During this chapter, Selena reads thirty-four books in four weeks. Why?

What was the "coolest" room that Selena has ever seen? Describe this room.

Why did Carla select number thirty-one when Joe Valentine asked all the kids to pick a number between one and 100?

ESSAY

Joe Valentine is shown as a role model to Selena in Chapter 5. What is a role model? Name someone in your life who has motivated you to achieve great things. Describe how this person helped you.

Chapter 6: Nobody's Perfect

When Selena returned to softball, what newly developed skill of hers shocked her teammates?

Why did Selena keep a picture of her mom in her back pocket when she took the mound?

Who was Victoria Joyce? What achievement of Selena's grabbed Victoria's attention?

ESSAY

Selena accomplishes a tremendous feat in this chapter by tossing a no-hitter. Detail a personal award, accomplishment, or honor in your life that makes you the most proud. Why are you so proud of this achievement?

Chapter 7: A Bumpy Ride

What life experiences did Selena and Victoria share that further strengthened their bond?

Give an example of how Coach Moody managed "by the book."

How did the softball team do under Coach Moody's direction?

ESSAY

In Chapter 7, Selena doesn't listen to Coach Moody and disrespects her in the process. Eventually, she learns to treat Coach Moody with respect, even though she doesn't always agree with her. Detail an example in your life when you disrespected someone. What lesson did you learn from it? Why is it important to respect people?

Chapter 8: Two Surprises

What is a quinceañera?

Why was Selena so excited about the news of the replacement softball coach?

What "tool" helped Selena the most in dealing with the pressures of playing softball?

ESSAY

Selena exhibits her resolve by not quitting the softball team in this chapter. Have you ever quit something in your life? Explain what happened. Why is finishing something you have started so important?

Chapter 9: Cinderella Superestrella

How did Selena hurt her ankle?

What lesson about pitching did Selena learn during her ankle rehabilitation?

Why did Selena refuse to wear her hair in bows, ribbons, or in a ponytail after her mother died?

ESSAY

In Chapter 9, when Selena injures her ankle, she manages to turn a bad situation into something positive. In fact, she becomes a more complete softball player after her injury. Detail a time in your life when you turned a negative situation into a positive one. What did you learn about yourself?

Chapter 10: Safe at Home

What news did Coach Lebot deliver to Selena in Victoria's office?

When was Selena's transformation to the sport of softball officially complete?

What did Selena leave beside her mother's tombstone when she visited the burial site?

ESSAY

Congratulations! You have completed another Scobre Press book! After joining Selena on her journey, detail what you learned from her life and experiences. How are you going to use Selena's story to help you achieve your dreams? What character traits does Selena have that could help you to overcome obstacles in your life?